POINT

DEAD RINGER

Dennis Hamley

■SCHOLASTIC

For Phil Levy and all the Pearse House staff

Scholastic Children's Books
Commonwealth House, 1–19 New Oxford Street,
London WC1A 1NU, UK
a division of Scholastic Ltd
London ~ New York ~ Toronto ~ Sydney ~ Auckland

First published in the UK by Scholastic Ltd, 1996

Copyright © Dennis Hamley, 1996

ISBN 0 590 13706 9

Typeset by TW Typesetting, Midsomer Norton, Avon
Printed by Cox & Wyman Ltd, Reading, Berks.

10 9 8 7 6 5 4 3 2 1

Prologue

*T*he Escort van was being driven fast along the narrow, hedgeless road through the bare Downs.

The headlights turned the short grass into a grey carpet. But stretching down the slope from the left was a white streak joining the road. This was really white, not an illusion in artificial light. The chalk track had been there centuries before the tarred road the van was taking; how many previous furtive and guilty scenes like the one it was host to now might have been played out on it?

The driver spoke. "Here. This is the ideal place. We'll get rid of it."

The passenger shuddered. If the driver noticed, he said nothing. The van stopped where the hard, dry track met the road. The driver switched the lights off.

"You see?" he said. "They'll find it here. And then they'll start thinking. 'Who did this?' they'll say. 'And why?' They'll come to the wrong answer. That's what the boss would want."

"Boss? You're the boss, aren't you?" said the passenger. New fears were dawning which made him even more appalled.

"You don't want to know," said the driver. "Forget I said that."

The van moved again. Lightless, it bumped along the track for a hundred metres, climbing until they were close to the summit of the Downs, where tracks of hooves scored the springy turf.

For a moment, the two sat side by side, not speaking. The passenger was still shaken by what had happened half an hour before.

"Did this one really deserve it?" he said.

"Of course. Anybody in our way deserves it. We've made a virtue out of necessity dumping it here. In fact it's a bit of a joke."

The passenger did not laugh.

"Let's get on with the job and be out of here. There's still work to do," said the driver.

They got out of the van and the driver opened the double door at the rear. The passenger climbed inside: then carefully lifted one end of the wrapped bundle. A shoeless foot protruded; the passenger quickly covered it with the white sheet. The driver had taken the body by the shoulders. Together they eased it out of the van and laid it gently on the short grass.

"Quick. Get back in," said the driver. The doors slammed. The van reversed down to the road. The head-lights shone forwards again and soon the Downs were quiet and deserted.

1

The early morning sun shone from a cloudless August sky. The horses, spurred on by their crouching riders, thundered across the downland.

Mornington Sunrise, a superb, dark brown three-year-old with a distinctive white blaze down his forehead, galloped easily, well within himself, at the rear of the ten-strong group. His rider knew he could urge him effortlessly faster; the rest would be overtaken as if they were little girls' ponies. But there was no need to do that. Mornington Sunrise was already a winner and going to be one of the great horses of the century. He should have won the Two Thousand Guineas and Derby that year already. Second in both wasn't good enough. That, everyone said, was all down to the jockey. But he'd win the year's last classic, the St Leger, no doubt of it. Remember the old adage – "a fit horse wins the

Guineas, a lucky horse the Derby, but the best horse wins the Leger." Well, Sunrise was simply the best.

So thought Nick Welsh as he felt the cool morning breeze flying past his face and the controlled power of the beast underneath him. Nick was seventeen, apprentice jockey at Johnny Rumbold-Straight's training stables near Matley village, here now for six months after his course at the British Racing School at Newmarket. Now they were all on the early-morning gallop across Matley Downs. That very morning, Johnny Rumbold-Straight, in his bluff, no-nonsense way, had barked at Nick: "Try Sunrise, lad. Have a change from the nags you're used to."

Johnny must have known the effect the invitation had on Nick. *I'm on the best. I've arrived. The guv'nor trusts me.*

So now he was savouring every second. And, because riding Mornington Sunrise was so *easy*, the horse so intelligent and responsive, he felt himself go half on auto-pilot. One part of his brain was precise, focused on the job in hand. The other drifted into thinking about the second great matter that was on his mind.

Margie. What was she playing at? Couldn't she see how he felt about her? Why did she have to taunt him like that? There'd been something wrong these last weeks. She'd avoided him, made excuses. Last night she'd been ill, husky voice over the phone, sore throat coming, so she couldn't see him.

So she said.

OK, Margie, I'd have taken that. But what a nasty shock was to follow. He'd gone into Salebourne with some of the lads, been in a few clubs. And there she was, in the Zero, dancing with this flash git. Designer haircut. Gold jewellery dripping off him. Looked as if he could buy the place out three times over. And she was laughing, long blonde hair bobbing, looking as if she fancied him rotten.

She hadn't seen Nick. And Nick hadn't told the others. But they'd seen something was wrong.

"You all right, mate?"

"Come on, loosen up."

But the evening was gone.

"I'm off home," said Nick. "Got to be up early tomorrow."

So he'd sat miserably on the bus back to Matley, wondering what he'd done wrong.

Well, not being rich and thirty for a start. No wonder this new one had turned Margie's head.

Why can't you wait, Margie? I'll be as big as Piggott or Swinburn one day. So he thought on the bus home.

And so he was thinking on this bright, breezy morning. *Sooner than you think if the boss puts me on horses like Mornington Sunrise.*

They were three-quarters through the gallop. Nick snapped back into full attention. Mornington Sunrise stayed easily, well within himself, at the rear of the pack. Nick allowed himself a quick look across the rolling downs, short grass, white gashes of old chalk quarries, the long white strip of a track cut across the

5

grass, the small white gash to his right as if someone had dug up turf to start cutting a new White Horse.

No, it wasn't a gash. It was something pale in colour lying on the ground.

A dead sheep?

No, too white.

Nick didn't know what made him rein Mornington Sunrise in, leave the main gallop, and walk in a wide circle around the object. Something: some premonition.

Johnny'll have my guts for garters, he thought. *So why am I doing it?*

No, it wasn't a sheep, but something wrapped in a white sheet.

Mornington Sunrise stopped, stood unconcerned. Nick was pleased he'd slowed his horse gently: no pulled muscles risked. But the horse was sweating; he should be covered at once. *Johnny will kill me*.

He nearly remounted and rode off. No, that would be stupid. Holding the reins in one hand, he bent gently to the bundle.

A thrill of horror ran through him. A human body.

He'd gone so far: he'd have to continue. Taking a deep breath, he twitched away the sheet where the head was.

And then he reeled, felt suddenly dizzy, let out a great howl and staggered for support against Mornington Sunrise. As if knowing his distress, the horse lowered his head and nuzzled Nick's neck.

The face was Margie's.

*　*　*

Nick had no idea how long he stood there, leaning against Mornington Sunrise's strong shoulder.

Margie had looked up at him, open blue eyes sightless. He couldn't bear the sight; he covered her with the sheet again, but the morning breeze kept blowing it back. There were marks on her neck. She must have been strangled. Why? Who?

Of course. That flash, gold-dripping git. Nick's fists clenched. *I'll get him. I won't wait for the police. I'll find out who he is and I'll get him myself.*

A noise interrupted him. A blue Range Rover was bumping over the grass towards him. Alf Simpkins drove, Johnny sat beside him, grim-faced. From fifty metres off, Nick heard Johnny's bellow.

"What the blazes do you think you're playing at?"

The Range Rover stopped. Johnny got out, red-faced with anger. He looked at Mornington Sunrise.

"Did he go lame?"

Nick shook his head.

"Thank the Lord for that. Greyling would have a fit."

Sir Norbury Greyling, multi-millionaire business tycoon, was Mornington Sunrise's owner.

At last, Johnny looked down at the bundle, just as the wind lifted the sheet again. He saw the dead face, the marks on the neck.

"My God," he said. "I know her. She lives in the village." Then, seeing Nick's stricken face, "She wasn't your...?"

Nick nodded.

Alf spoke.

"It's Margie Moxon, sir," he said. "You know her father. He owns the saddler's and tack shop."

"She was my girlfriend," Nick managed to stutter.

"Alf, get the horse back," said Johnny. "I'll stay here till the police come."

Alf nodded, took a horse-blanket from the back of the Range Rover and threw it over Mornington Sunrise. Then he led the horse away.

"Take your helmet off," said Johnny gently.

Nick did so and felt the breeze ruffle his hair. The sun was climbing: the day would be warm.

"Nothing for it," said Johnny. "The police will have to hear."

He pulled his mobile phone from the holster on his belt and dialled 999.

"Police," he barked. Then, "Urgent. On the Downs at the end of the training gallop. Up from where the old track crosses the Matley-Salebourne road. There's a body here. Looks like murder."

"Tell them I know who did it," said Nick.

Johnny did no such thing.

"This is Rumbold-Straight. Yes, I'll be here. So will my apprentice who found it."

He put the phone back. "What do you mean, you know who did it?"

"I saw them both last night in the Zero. He was a wrong 'un – all his bracelets and medallions. And his haircut would cost me a week's wages. He *did* it."

"What was his name?" said Johnny.

"I don't know. I'd never seen him before."

"Just as well. I don't want you taking the law into your own hands."

"But I'll find him."

"Let the police do their job for a change." Johnny's opinion of the local force was not high.

Nick, for all the increasing warmth, shivered.

"Go on, lad," said Johnny. "Sit in the Range Rover."

Dumbly, Nick climbed into the passenger seat. He sank back into its capacious comfort. Then, without being able to stop himself and not even caring if Johnny saw him, he burst into tears. They coursed down his face uncontrollably at the thought that he would never see Margie again or hear her laughing voice, feel her kiss, watch her yellow hair gleam and ripple as she walked.

Nick had no idea how long it was before he looked out of the Range Rover's window and saw they were surrounded by police cars and the area round the body was sealed off with tape. Two photographers were moving all round Margie's body, clicking away from every angle. Police were combing the area, vainly seeking incriminating objects on the short grass.

A man detached himself from the scrum; Nick could see him talking to Johnny. They both looked towards the Range Rover. The man, youngish,

9

dressed in a short leather topcoat and grey trousers, came across and knocked on the window.

Nick opened the door.

"Detective-Inspector Chase," said the man. "Nick Welsh?" Nick nodded. "I understand you found the body."

"I know who killed her. Why don't you get him?" Nick burst out.

"Hold hard," said Inspector Chase. "Calm down and tell me how you found her."

Nick did so.

"I don't understand. Why did you stop?" demanded the Inspector. "You were riding a thoroughbred horse on a training gallop. You've upset your horse's routine and fallen down on your job because, according to what you've just told me, you first thought you were looking at a dead sheep. Why didn't you finish and tell Mr Rumbold-Straight what you'd seen, so you could all go back and look properly?"

Nick looked at him open-mouthed. Yes, why not?

Inspector Chase looked at him narrowly and shrewdly.

"I'd almost think you *knew* what you were going to find," he said.

"No!" Nick yelped.

"Then why?" Inspector Chase persisted.

A premonition, a gut feeling, a sinking of the stomach, an instinct that he had to stop? Nick told the Inspector these things, ending with, "Margie was my girlfriend."

"Ah!" said the Inspector. "Now we're getting somewhere."

"And I saw her last night in the Zero Club with this rich guy."

"So jealousy made you psychic?" said Inspector Chase. There was a note of sarcasm Nick didn't like.

"*He's* the man who killed her. Get him. Don't keep on at me," he shouted.

"Calm down," said Inspector Chase. "We'll find him. I don't believe you expected to see the body of Margie Moxon. But I do think your subconscious was on the lookout for signs of something. And I want you to think hard, and when you've thought, I want you round at the station to tell me."

Nick could see, behind the Inspector, Margie's body lifted, put on a stretcher, covered and slid into the back of a police van.

"What about the man who killed her?" he cried.

"Full description, please," said Inspector Chase.

Nick thought back to the hot, noisy scene in half-light. Margie was vivid in his eyes – but the stranger?

"About six feet, short designer haircut, dark, thin, tanned, white open-necked shirt, black leather trousers, gold medallion, gold bracelets."

"Age?"

Nick thought. His sort could be anything from twenty-five to fifty.

"Could be any age," he admitted.

"So we're looking for one of the regular, middle-aged, over-sexed swingers who haunt these clubs in

their thousands," said Inspector Chase. "Well, we'll
have a go."

He turned to where Johnny stood waiting.

"He's all yours," he said. "Take him home."

As they swung off the road through the gates into the
stables, Johnny said, "You've had a shock. Take the
day off."

Nick had never heard his voice so gentle.

"Thanks," he said.

Yes, he needed some time to himself.

He jumped out of the Range Rover and crossed to
the tack room. As he was changing back into
ordinary clothes, Alf walked in.

"So he's let you off, has he?"

Did Alf mean the Inspector or Johnny?

"Well, I wouldn't have. Work's the best healer."

Surly old twerp, thought Nick. Still, as head lads
went, Alf wasn't too bad. (What daft tradition still
called a man of fifty a *lad*?) At least you knew where
you stood with Alf.

Soon he was in Matley High Street. The village
had well woken up, but over the noise of people and
parking cars, Nick heard a voice shrilling out.

"Nick. Wait for me."

He turned.

A fresh-faced girl his own age ran down the pave-
ment towards him. Her brown hair was cut short and
she wore jeans and shirt.

Karen Thorpe. The last person he wanted to face.

"Nick. There's rumours all over the village. About Margie. They can't be true, can they?"

Karen wasn't exactly a pain but … well, she worked with Margie in the Moxons' saddlery and had always lived in the village – unlike Nick, who, like the rest of the apprentices, lived in digs – was fanatic about horses, wanted to be a jockey, couldn't see why she shouldn't be apprenticed like Nick was and NEVER SHUT UP ABOUT IT.

And she fancied him. He knew that for a fact. And once he'd given her cause to— Oh, forget that now. But she was never sniffing round now to see if he was free, surely?

No, that's not right. Forget you thought that as well.

"Yes, it's true," he said.

"Tell me what happened. Let's go and have a coffee."

"Why aren't you at work?" said Nick.

"My day off," Karen replied.

The expensive restaurants, hotels and pubs to serve the rich racing folk weren't open yet and Karen and Nick wouldn't have gone in one if they had been. They slipped into a greasy-spoon café at the end of the street and drank tasteless coffee amid smells of frying bacon.

"Poor Nick," said Karen. "And poor Margie. Tell all."

Once again, Nick poured the whole story out. Karen listened, wincing sometimes, saying nothing.

Until the end. Then she spoke. "The designer man in the Zero. You know who he is, don't you?"

"No idea. Never seen him before."

"Well, I do. And I'll tell you where to find him."

2

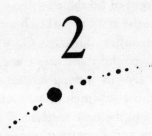

Inspector Chase drove reflectively back to the police station in Salebourne. They needed an incident room closer to the murder. After a quick call on the car-phone in the Range Rover, his superintendent was even now commandeering a disused chapel in Matley which would be ideal. New phone lines would be laid in and computers set up. Meanwhile, his mind was troubled. Not by the sight of Margie's body though, he had seen too many corpses over the years to turn a hair. No, there were other things which were odd.

That young apprentice jockey, for a start, so upset and so sure about who had done it. Well, discount that for a start: he'd heard too many jealous lovers shouting their mouths off to be impressed. But this morning had been different. He'd liked Nick on sight, and felt sorry for the shocked, grief-stricken and gobsmacked lad.

And the body itself, so carefully wrapped up and deposited in the middle of nowhere. Ah, but was it? Could the main morning gallop of top horses be called the middle of nowhere?

He reached the station, parked his car and walked upstairs to his office. Through the window he saw the Range Rover and more cars come into the yard from Matley Downs, having left an army of constables to comb every inch of surrounding ground. He rang down to the desk sergeant.

"Tell Kemp and Ruggles to come up as soon as they're here."

Sergeant Kemp and Detective-Constable Ruggles were both older than whizz-kid Inspector Chase. He valued them and wished they didn't think he was some young upstart telling them their jobs. Because he wouldn't. They were too good for that.

There was a knock on the door. The two entered – Kemp, sandy-haired and in his forties, wearing a sober sports jacket; Ruggles, hardly thirty, in jeans. They sat in front of his desk.

"Well, what do you make of it?" he said.

The two looked at each other. Kemp cleared his throat.

"At the moment, sir, not a lot," he said.

"The search won't be any good," said Ruggles. "It's all chalk up there: no footprints or tyre tracks and those blasted flying hooves have probably trampled over anything else."

"So where do we start?" said Chase.

"What did you make of the boy who found her?" said Kemp. "Nick Welsh, wasn't it?"

"He has to go to number one on our list," said Chase. "She was his girlfriend, she was obviously two-timing him and he'd only found out the night before. And how many murders of young women do you know that were done by exactly such a person?"

The other two were silent, knowing the number was very high.

"So shall we bring him in?" said Ruggles.

"Not yet. I'm still not happy."

"I can see why," said Kemp. "I don't know about you but if I'd topped my girlfriend in a fit of jealous rage I'd have either run off in panic and left her there or, if I kept my cool, tried to dump her in the river, under the floorboards or dig a hole in the garden. Anything to make sure she wasn't found for a while. I *wouldn't* wrap her in a white sheet, take her miles in the country and drop her in the path of twenty thundering racehorses where she's bound to be found first thing next morning."

"Exactly," said Chase.

"Isn't it strange, then, about *who* found her?" said Ruggles.

"Exactly, once again," said Chase. "Another reason to be unhappy."

"So is the place her murderer chose to leave her significant?" said Kemp.

"She was left there for young Welsh to find," said Ruggles.

"Possibly," said Chase. "We might know more when we get the pathologist's report."

"The girl's father keeps the tack shop. The boy is an apprentice jockey in stables. Everyone's to do with horses," said Kemp.

"*Everything's* to do with damned horses in Matley," said Chase. "That worries me as well."

"I know," said Ruggles feelingly.

"Everyone from down-and-outs to royalty gets into racing. Ruined gamblers, unscrupulous bookies, jockeys pumped up full of adrenalin, trainers only as secure as the next big win so the rich owners don't take their horses away; the great, the good, the not-so good and the downright evil all with their snouts in the trough, from lottery winners through old football stars to big business, royalty and peers of the realm, most with a few dark secrets to hide. I groan when something comes up at Matley: will this be the can of worms I've dreaded all my life when I might have to point my finger at very dangerous, powerful people who think they're above the law?"

Kemp and Ruggles looked at each other and smiled. They'd been here longer than Chase.

"Glad you're cottoning on, sir," said Detective-Constable Ruggles.

Nick stared at Karen.

"Who do you mean?" he said.

"You won't believe this. He lives with his mum in Salebourne."

"How do you know?"

Karen looked at the table and fiddled with the teaspoon before she answered.

"Margie told me about him," she said.

Nick couldn't believe this. For a moment he was beyond speech – whether with anger over Margie's duplicity, or shame about his rejection, a joke in women's conversation he couldn't share.

Karen seemed to understand. She laid a hand on his arm.

"Don't worry," she said. "It's not like you think. She said he was a prat."

"Then why bother with him?"

"Ted Firs was a giggle. She was taking the mickey out of him."

Nick remembered the leather trousers, the medallion, gold jewellery, expensively-cut shirt. That outfit was not cheap. Nor was his haircut.

"He *dripped* with money," he said. "I knew Margie, warts and all. She wouldn't go over the top *just* for a rich guy."

"But she said he wasn't. He'd got money suddenly – a lot, it seems. She didn't ask how. Well, you don't, do you? And who is it who gets a bit of money and straight away turns himself into medallion man?"

"I don't know," said Nick.

"Well, I'll tell you. It's your thickhead. And do you know what most girls would do when they find a rich thick? Get all they can and take him for a ride before they dump him."

Nick looked hard at Karen with her soft brown eyes.

"You wouldn't," he said.

"No, but Margie might."

Nick looked down at the check table–cloth and felt tears stinging his eyes again. He tried hard not to believe these new views on Margie.

"Look where it got her," he said at last.

Karen rose.

"Come on," she said. "I told you I knew where you could find him. I'll come with you, so you won't murder him yourself."

At Johnny Rumbold-Straight's stables, the important business could not wait. The horses were in the stables, rubbed down, groomed, fed. The stable-lads – minus Nick – were busy keeping the place clean. Alf Simpkins was sorting out the transportation to take six horses to Buckingham the following week and eight others to Bishop's Stortford a fortnight after for big meetings at both racecourses. Mornington Sunrise was entered for the Gawcott Stakes at Buckingham and the Puckeridge Cup at Bishop's Stortford – important races both, but no classics, and for him merely training runs in his build-up for the St Leger in September.

Alf was ordering a six-box transporter for the Buckingham meeting and a nine-box for Bishop's Stortford from Matley Racehorse Transport. To his intense annoyance, Mornington Sunrise would not be on either of these conveyances. Sir Norbury Greyling insisted the horse always travelled alone in a luxurious box kept at the stables for his exclusive use – and Alf was always to drive it, with hand-picked second drivers and attendants. Well, Sir Norbury, boss of Kudic plc, vast worldwide business conglomerate, among the world's richest men, could probably afford to be picky.

Johnny himself stood in the yard watching his team at work. Yes, he'd built up a good business, with a sky-high reputation. Top owners, top horses, top jockeys. Plenty of classic winners. A marvellous record at lesser meetings. But never the Derby or Leger. Oh, how he'd love to. That would be the icing on his already rich cake. He could die happy on the spot.

He looked over to Mornington Sunrise's stable. That long, wise, intelligent head looked back at him; the horse was entirely unfazed by his morning's adventure. Johnny had had good horses, *great* horses through his stables in the past. But never a beast like Mornington Sunrise. For a moment he returned Sunrise's gaze and felt he was having a silent convers-ation with the most intelligent creature in the county.

Then he shook his head, snapped out of his day-dream. Something had happened which could cost them all dear. Johnny could smell a crisis a mile off.

"Alf," he shouted. "In my office. Now."

"Coming, sir," came a voice from behind an open window over a stable. Alf emerged from his tiny office and followed his boss.

* * *

Inspector Chase was talking to the pathologist.

"So there's not much to be gained," he said.

"Not a lot," said Dr Gregson. "Dead, I'd say, between eleven p.m. and one in the morning. Strangled, probably by bare, very strong, large hands. No disarrangement of clothing, no sign of any other assault. I don't know – I get a strange feeling…"

His voice tailed off.

"Go on," said Chase.

"Well, I'm sure there was no sex motive here. That's odd in itself. Late at night, she'd been in a club, a few drinks down her, she was a terrific-looking girl – yet her killing seems totally clinical. And then there's the sheet she was wrapped in."

"Yes?" Chase felt sudden hope.

"Nothing much. Except for one stain on it. Motor oil. Castrol, Shell, something like that. We can have it analysed."

"Oh, big deal," said Chase bitterly. "Almost every sump in every car in the country's filled with the stuff."

"Well, that's it, for what it's worth. I'll have it all typed up for you."

Chase left, pondering. Then – *but, of course*, he thought. It's something. Margie Moxon could have been murdered in a garage.

Alf stood in Johnny's huge office. Johnny Rumbold-Straight might look from the outside like a red-faced, whisky-soaked hearty but – as Alf was well aware – he knew exactly how to get what he wanted. Or was it all through Connie, his wife? Connie and Johnny: they operated together, a formidable pairing. A thick, pale green carpet, a vast desk of Norwegian pine, light beige walls, deep armchairs, a trophy case full of polished silverware, bookshelves lined with expensive bindings (and not for show: Alf knew well there was enough racing lore packed between those covers to rival any library), big double-glazed windows, a drinks cabinet stocked full of the best... Johnny had built a little working palace for himself, carefully calculated, probably by Connie, to awe his employees, make jockeys know they rode for someone worthwhile and convince owners they had brought their horses to the right place. After he had passed through the outer office, greeted Beryl Lackland sitting behind her word processor next to the filing cabinets and entered this place, Alf always felt a mixture of awe, and pride in his employer.

So it was now. Johnny leaned back in his chair, waved towards an armchair and said, "Don't stand on ceremony, Alf. Get your bum parked."

Alf sat diffidently, worried about the breeches he'd supervised the mucking-out in.

"Alf," said Johnny. "You don't think that business this morning has anything to do with us, do you?"

"I don't see how it can, sir," said Alf. "There's no connection between Margie Moxon and the stables."

"Except young Nick having the hots for her, it

seems. Well, if that was the case, everywhere would be connected with everywhere else, I suppose."

"It was just coincidence she was dumped on a training run our horses were using," said Alf.

"I hope so," said Johnny. "I don't want the police round here and I especially don't want reporters sniffing round making something of nothing. There's been bad press about places like ours lately: trainers shot, doping scandals, licences lost. I don't want it here. I want people seeing me on television with Derby winners. I don't want the Duke of Rothley and Sheikh Naseem Ali taking their horses away. Nor even Billy Boney." Alf winced at the memory of the zany comedian, owner of three good horses and shrewd behind the demented exterior. "And what if Sir Norbury took Mornington Sunrise over to Ireland?"

"Or to Kiteley," said Alf.

Johnny ground his teeth with anger at the name. Arthur Kiteley ran a racing stable the other side of the village. He and Johnny had hated each other for years.

"Look, sir," said Alf. He might only be head lad but he knew Johnny depended a lot on his experience and judgement. "This will soon be cleared up. They say Margie put herself about a bit. Young Welsh was about the only one who couldn't see it. She got some poor chap fired up a bit more than she bargained for and paid the price. The police will find him before the week's out."

"I hope so, for all our sakes," said Johnny. Then, rarely sentimental – "And especially young Nick Welsh's sake. I don't want him upset now. He's good. I've got plans for him."

"I was going to talk to you about that," said Alf.

Karen and Nick got off the bus in Salebourne city centre.

"Now where?" said Nick.

She led him away from the shops, the Cathedral, the riverside cafés, down quiet streets where houses became smaller and less prosperous.

"How do you know this Ted Firs anyway?" asked Nick.

"I was out with Margie in Salebourne months ago. Well, this Ted Firs tried to get off with us. Honestly, Nick, you should have seen him. He looked like the village idiot. And when we'd sent him packing they told us he nearly was."

"Really?"

"Put it this way. A Salebourne girl told me he was a nuisance but harmless, fivepence short of a pound coin."

"Margie never told me. And he didn't look harmless to me. Or gormless. And where did he get it all from, then?"

"I don't know. Perhaps he won the lottery?"

"I just can't believe Margie would go off with a dickhead."

"Perhaps it was all that sudden money."

"Oh, no, not Margie. Not *just* for that."

"Well, he found some way of impressing her. We'll soon find out. Carver Street. This is it."

They turned a corner into a street lined on both sides with small, old terraced houses, some with new bay windows built on. At the end the road came up suddenly against a fence. On the other side was the railway. Even as they watched, a train shot past towards London.

Karen led Nick to the last house. Outside was a Ford Capri, gleaming and well-restored.

"The Basildon Lamborghini," said Nick. "Just the car medallion man would drive."

"Knock at the door," said Karen.

Nick opened the gate of the tiny front garden and banged the knocker on the green front door, badly in need of new paint.

No answer.

He peered through the front window.

"It doesn't look as if his mum's in either," said Karen.

At the end of the terrace, this house had a passage round the side into the back garden. They walked round, on to an unkempt lawn of scruffy tufts of grass. Nick knocked on the kitchen door.

No answer again.

He looked through the kitchen window. No sign of life.

He turned to Karen. "All flown the nest," he said.

"Let's look up the garden," she said.

Beyond the lawn there were just a few straggly cabbages and Brussels sprouts. At the very end was a brick wall with a wooden gate set into it, leading to an alleyway allowing all the houses to have back entrances. Nick looked through and up and down the alleyway.

A train clattered past, slowing to stop at Salebourne.

And then Nick called to Karen in a small, frightened, choked voice. She came to him and they looked down at the ground just inside the gate, and between the wall and a broken garden frame.

They had found Ted Firs, in his leather trousers, medallion and gold jewellery twinkling, sprawled out with blood congealed round his head, staring skywards. He seemed still puzzled by what was happening to him even though he was by now long dead.

3

"**Y**ou again!" said Inspector Chase.

Nick felt a sudden sinking of the heart. Dead bodies were littering his life. He knew he was in for hours with the police before they'd believe they were nothing to do with him.

Inspector Chase had just gone over with Kemp and Ruggles to the new incident room in Matley when the message reached him. A 999 call: the dead man was the very same seen last night with the dead woman. So they left for Carver Street.

"Looks like we'll need two incident rooms," said Ruggles, as he drove the siren-blasting Rover.

"I fancy not," said Chase. "Lightning rarely strikes twice. These murders will be connected."

When he saw Nick Welsh with yet another girl-friend, he was sure. Resisting the temptation to say to her, "Get out of his life, love. He attracts corpses.

The next might be yours," he just looked at Nick and said, "You again!"

And Nick saw a wealth of unpleasant meaning in those words.

That morning, unannounced, a grey Rolls-Royce turned into the yard. A uniformed chauffeur got out, spoke to Alf. Alf looked aghast, then ran off to Johnny's office.

Johnny Rumbold-Straight was aghast too. The news of Margie's body on the training gallop had reached local radio and now television. The phone was ringing with calls from newspapers as well as nervous owners. With a sinking heart, Johnny realized they were in for a hard time.

Alf was about to make him even more horrified. He bounded up the stairs and shouted to Beryl. "Is he in? I've got to see him."

Beryl lifted the phone to warn Johnny, then said, "What's happened, Alf? Has the roof fallen in?"

"As good as," Alf gulped and burst into the office. He stood panting in front of Johnny. "Greyling's here," he said.

Johnny's head went straight into his hands.

"That's all I need," he groaned. There were three owners Johnny was determined not to upset: Sheikh Naseem Ali, the Duke of Rothley and, most of all, Sir Norbury. If others took their horses away he could repair the breach. Any one of these, then the other two would follow, word would spread like wildfire and he'd be finished.

"Checking up on Sunrise," muttered Johnny. Then, out loud, "Make yourself scarce, Alf. Be ready for an inspection. I don't have to ask if his horses will be perfect: I know they will. Out of the back door, quick, and rouse those lads of yours."

Then he rose, left the office, said to Beryl, "Get drinks ready for Sir Norbury. You know what he likes. It's never too early for him. Or me when he turns up without notice and catches me on the hop," and trod heavily down the stairs.

The team was combing the garden and the alleyway and knocking on front doors in Carver Street. There was a question to settle first.

"Did either of you open the back gate of the Firs' house?" asked Sergeant Kemp.

"I did," said Nick. "From inside the yard."

"Right. Now, be careful about this. Did you have to unbolt it or was it just left on the latch?"

Nick thought. Yes, he was sure. "I didn't have to slip the bolts," he said. "I was a bit surprised about that. Anyone could have come in from the alley."

"Good. Thank you," said Kemp.

Nick continued helpfully. "You'll know when you find my fingerprints on the latch," he said.

Kemp gazed at him thoughtfully.

"We've been doing this job for a few years now, son," he said.

No one answered the bangs on the door and the

shouts of "Open up". So, at a nod from Chase, Ruggles delicately felt in Ted Firs' pockets and brought out a bunch of keys: a Yale, an ordinary door key and a car key.

The Yale fitted the front door, the other key the back. One minute later, the police knew the house was empty. No multiple murder waiting for them inside. A minute after that and the news came from next door: Ted's mother had gone to stay with her sister.

"Get the number and bring her back," said Chase to a WPC. "And take these two away" – pointing to Nick and Karen. "I want to talk to them very seriously."

The car key fitted the Capri; two policemen were now scouring the inside. Chase, Kemp and Ruggles looked at the body.

"What do you think?" said Chase.

"I don't reckon he was killed here," said Ruggles. "No sign of a struggle, no blood anywhere except on his head, so it had congealed before he ended upon the ground just there." He looked with distaste at the sprawled body.

"The inside of the house is as neat as a pin," said Kemp. "Just what a house-proud woman would leave before she went away. No violent assaults there. He was killed somewhere else."

"Like Margie Moxon," said Chase.

"The same people?" asked Ruggles.

"Has to be," said Chase.

"So did he struggle along nearly dead back to his own home, open the gate he'd left conveniently unbolted and finally give out by the wall?" said Ruggles.

"And carefully shut the gate behind him? No chance," said Chase. "He was brought here, I'm sure. Probably along the back alley."

"There's hardly room for a car to get along," Kemp pointed out. "And they'd make a heck of a noise reversing out."

The photographing and measuring of the body was complete. Ted Firs' remains were picked up, put on a trolley, and covered. As the first stage of Ted's journey to the mortuary and a full examination started, Dr Gregson took off his gloves, wiped his glasses and came to Chase.

"Dead since the early hours of this morning, I'd say," he said. "Just like the other one. Heavy blow to the back of the head. No other immediate signs of injury. A very *simple* death, I think."

"Here or somewhere else?"

"Oh, come, that's for you to find out, not the humble medic," said Gregson, and left with the body in the same van that a few hours earlier had carried Margie Moxon.

"Tell Forensic," said Chase to Kemp, "that as well as anything else they find, I want the oil stain on the sheet covering Margie checked out first, urgently, to see if there's anything similar on Ted's gear. And anything else which suggests they might have met their ends in a garage."

"And now what?" said Kemp.

"Back to the Matley incident room. We're staying there because I've got a feeling Matley's where the answers are. We'll soon hear what turned up in the house-to-house. And we've got to talk to our two young friends."

Sir Norbury Greyling sat heavily in an armchair. Beryl Lackland came in at Johnny's call and set up a decanter of malt whisky. Johnny poured him a large measure in a chunky glass. Only when Sir Norbury was fully settled did Johnny risk sitting behind his desk.

Silence. Johnny, not easily intimidated, felt intimidated now by this mega-rich, powerful man. Finally, Sir Norbury spoke.

"There's been a murder here."

"Not here," said Johnny. Alf would have been amazed at the stutter in his voice. "On the Downs, on the training gallop."

"*Here*," said Sir Norbury firmly. "Found on *your* gallop, by one of *your* employees riding *my* horse, so *here*."

Johnny looked at the stern, craggy face, the beetling eyebrows. He felt the awesome power of great wealth. He had no answer. It crossed his mind to wonder how Sir Norbury *knew* so soon. He could only think of one possibility. Arch-enemy Kiteley, on the phone straight away, causing maximum trouble.

"I will not have any horse of mine surrounded

by notoriety-attracting publicity," continued Sir Norbury. "There will be no such further incidents."

"But I have no control..." Johnny stutteringly began.

"No notice will be paid to my horses by the world at large except when they win."

Johnny found a voice. "But this will die down," he said. "A little tart murdered and dumped; sheer coincidence that the body was found by Mornington Sunrise's rider – nothing to do with the horse at all. The police will soon have the killer."

Sir Norbury leaned back and surveyed Johnny.

"I have become rich by smelling danger a long way off," he said. "And I know when to avoid it and when to go out and meet it head on. The stench of danger is here. I don't know why; I don't know what it is – but smell it I do, stinking, fetid, repulsive. It is to be avoided. I have made up my mind what to do."

Johnny waited miserably, seeing Mornington Sunrise and six other terrific horses being loaded into boxes on their way to Ireland – or, shorter but more terribly, the three mile journey to Arthur Kiteley. And his reputation being led away with them.

"You have done a good job," said Sir Norbury. "No one could have done better." Johnny braced himself for the "But..."

It never came. "I do not want to break continuity or put my horses to greater risk. I therefore intend to put my own man in here. He will live over the stables, he will be present at all dealings with my horses, he will travel on the boxes when they go to meetings. He will especially accompany Mornington Sunrise."

"Instead of Alf?" asked Johnny. Most others, even the Duke of Rothley and especially Billy Boney, would have been asked to take their horses away rather than impose such a condition. But other owners would never dream of it – and even Sheikh Naseem didn't have half Sir Norbury's clout. Johnny would have to accept gracefully and treat it as prudence, not insult.

"As well as Simpkins," said Sir Norbury. "My man is skilled with horses, he is an expert in security and a first-rate driver. I won't foist a drone on you. He will arrive this afternoon. Suitable quarters will be prepared for him at once. You may tell Simpkins, but no one else is to know. As far as others are concerned, you have taken on a new stable-lad."

Sir Norbury relaxed.

"And now, tell me about Mornington Sunrise. Is he on course for the St Leger?"

Johnny nearly ducked out of his next remark. But, no, he had to stand his ground.

"Alf and I have been talking," he said. "We want to put a young apprentice up on him for the Gawcott Stakes at Buckingham."

"Why?" said Sir Norbury, suddenly frosty again. Mornington Sunrise's usual jockey was the veteran Paddy O'Keefe, champion jockey three times already.

"O'Keefe's past his best," said Johnny. "Sunrise hasn't reached his yet. Besides, Kiteley has offered O'Keefe a bigger retainer than I'm prepared to pay him."

"I pay you for your good judgement so I must trust it," said Sir Norbury. "Who do you have in mind?"

"Nick Welsh."

"The name is familiar. How good is he?"

"First-rate. Good seat, marvellous hands, brave as a lion on a horse, though a bit soft when he's off one. If I'm not watching a great jockey in the making, I'm not fit to run stables."

"I believe you, of course. Can I see him ride now?"

Johnny cleared his throat. "That's a bit difficult. I gave him the day off. He's had a bit of a shock."

Sir Norbury stood up, anger suffusing his face. *Another crisis*, Johnny inwardly groaned. *The times are all against me*.

"I knew his name was familiar. He's the one who found the body. He's part of the bad publicity."

"Yes," admitted Johnny.

Sir Norbury's brow cleared. He sat down again.

"Well, I suppose it's not his fault. I'll take your word for it – and about his talent."

Johnny poured Sir Norbury more whisky, and one for himself. They drank silently, reflectively. Then Sir Norbury rose.

"Take me to my horses," he said.

Johnny stood as well. He was happy. He had stood

his ground. He had taken a knock early on but he had got his own way and in the end, by announcing Nick was to ride Sir Norbury's greatest horse, had scored a point with a sneaky jab. Well, one of the keys to being a successful trainer was to stand up to the rich and famous. And he'd done just that with the richest of the lot.

They walked downstairs together into the bright sunshine.

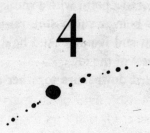

4

If Sir Norbury Greyling had known where his new jockey was he might not have been so happy. Nick and Karen had been taken to Matley in separate cars and then put in separate rooms.

Karen found herself with Sergeant Kemp and a WPC. She looked scared stiff. The WPC tried to put her at her ease and Sergeant Kemp was gentle in his questioning.

"Just tell me why you were where we found you with Nick Welsh?"

So Karen went through it all again.

"I saw Nick in the village. There were rumours about Margie flying round and I wanted to know if they were true. So I went with Nick for a coffee and he told me they were and all about the man he saw Margie with last night. I told him I knew who he was and Nick said he wanted me to take him there so he could have it all out with him."

"And you found Ted Firs dead?"

"Yes."

"A complete shock?"

Karen shuddered. "Yes."

"Did it occur to you that once Nick told you what he suspected of a person you could identify, your proper course was to contact us?"

"No, it didn't."

"Or that Welsh might be so angry that he might kill Firs himself? Or that Firs might assault him?"

"Never. Nick wouldn't. And poor Ted was harmless. He was thick."

"Nick's description of him to my inspector didn't paint a very savoury picture. But it didn't make him seem thick."

"Ted Firs dressed himself up. But he was still thick."

"And you knew him but Nick didn't."

"I didn't really *know* him. I'd *seen* him, heard about him."

"You knew him enough to know Margie was carrying on with him."

"She told me about him. She was just taking him for a ride."

"How well do you know Nick?"

Karen didn't answer. Kemp read the silence.

"I get the picture. Correct me if I'm wrong, but wasn't it a case of Nick fancying Margie and you fancying Nick?"

Again, no answer. Kemp took that as confirmation.

"Wouldn't it have been nicer to *tell* Nick about Margie instead of letting him find out for himself?"

"It was none of my business. And I'm no sneak," said Karen.

"So you let him carry on in his fool's paradise."

"He'd have been furious with me if I'd told him. He wouldn't have believed it. And then I'd have had *no* chance."

"It might have saved two lives," said Kemp.

Silence again. Then Karen spoke wearily. "What was the point? Margie was only stringing him along. But Nick would never have believed that."

Kemp changed the subject. "Have you got a job?"

"I work in Margie's father's saddler's shop."

"No wonder you know all about Margie."

"She was my best friend."

"Did you see her father this morning?"

"No. Today's my day off."

"Very convenient. So you work in a saddler's. That's working with horses in a way."

"Everybody works with horses in Matley."

"And the saddler's shop's where you want to stay until Mr Right comes along. Is that it?"

"No," said Karen fiercely. "I want to be a jockey. A real female jockey."

"There are quite a few already."

"Oh, no. Not like I want to be. They're still looked on like they're freaks. I want to be seen as a good jockey in my own right, just as much as Paddy O'Keefe is or Nick will be."

"But nobody lets you. Is that it?"

"Mr Rumbold-Straight won't take me on." Karen's voice was angry. "He won't take on *any* girls. They say he's too afraid of Connie."

"But I've heard about girls working in racing stables."

"I don't just want to muck the horses out. I want to *ride* them. I'm not spending my time being got at by that chauvinist lot. I want to *be* somebody there."

"Well, the best of luck to you. But Rumbold-Straight's not the only trainer round here. What about Arthur Kiteley?"

Silence again. Then, with great finality, "No."

Kemp said nothing for a few moments, but studied her carefully, as if trying to sum her up. Finally, he spoke.

"I reckon you'd do anything to get what you want," he said.

"What do you mean?" said Karen.

"Forget it," said Kemp. "You can go now."

Surprised at this sudden ending, Karen left to wait for Nick.

Nick's interview was longer. Chase and Ruggles saw him.

"This is getting to be a habit," said Chase. "Two dead bodies in one morning and you've found both. To say the least, it looks odd."

"Of course it's odd," said Nick. "It's flaming weird."

"No more than that? Think carefully. You see, we don't like coincidences in the detective game."

"Of *course* it's coincidence," Nick shouted. "I don't know anything about either murder. I didn't know Ted Firs."

"But Margie did. And so, it seems, did Karen. Doesn't it bother you, all these girls going round keeping secrets? First rule if you want to reach your natural span – never trust a woman."

Nick shifted uncomfortably but said nothing.

Inspector Chase continued. "This morning I said I didn't think you killed Margie. And if you didn't, it's unlikely you were around to kill Firs. We'll soon check on that. What did you do after you saw Margie in the Zero Club?"

"Went back to Matley on the ten-fifteen bus from Salebourne."

"Who saw you?"

"The driver. There were a few passengers. I didn't know them."

"We'll check. Then what?"

"I went to my digs in Matley."

Nick, with three other stable-lads, lodged in a guest house kept by Mr and Mrs Fanshaw.

"You were seen there?"

"Oh, yes."

"If it all checks out, you're in the clear. But I still don't think this is coincidence."

"What do you mean?"

"You're involved in these murders whether you

like it or not. I don't know how but I mean to find out. Let's start again. You really didn't know Firs?"

"Never heard of him."

"So everybody seems to have known him, but you."

"I've only been here six months."

"And now your girlfriend and the man you wanted to get even with for pinching her off you end up violently dead at the same time and you find both bodies. You're involved all right. Now, let's think about your subconscious for a while, shall we?"

"How?" said Nick.

"Just think. Any little thing you remember which could connect with this – about Margie, Karen, anyone you've come into contact with over the last few weeks. Anything in your job at the stables, at a race meeting you've been to. Anything at all which seems out of the ordinary."

Nick was silent. Nothing had prepared him for the two rocking shocks he had received that morning.

Yet he knew the Inspector had read him like a book. There *was* something in his brain, some little circumstance, which had made him not *entirely* surprised at that terrible moment when he had lifted the sheet and seen Margie's dead face. It wasn't just a sixth sense: it was something he *knew* and had forgotten. Or didn't want to remember. If he would just bring himself to *say* it, things might end up a lot easier.

Or would they? They might be worse.

Minutes passed. Nothing.

In the end, Inspector Chase said, almost gently, "All right, give up, Nick. It will come when you least expect it. Just let me know when, will you?"

They let him go and he joined Karen outside.

They stood together in Matley High Street. Just down the road was the greasy spoon where only a few hours before, though it seemed days, Karen had told Nick about Ted Firs. To their left, the street widened into the old market place; the parking spaces where stalls used to be were full of Range Rovers and Mercedes. The racing folk of Matley had come to eat and drink. Behind the hotel doors and inn-signs, inside the lovely old buildings, the bars would be full.

Karen suddenly took Nick's hand and squeezed it.

"I hate this place," she said. "Let's start our day again."

Nick didn't answer. So Karen led him to the bus stop. They stood there, Karen still gripping his un-responsive hand.

"You look shell-shocked," she said. "It wasn't that bad in there, was it?"

"He told me to think back," said Nick. "He says I know something important and I've forgotten it. So I'm trying. But it's no good."

Margie's dead face hovered in his mind.

"But he's right," he said. "There *is* something. What *is* it?"

The bus was coming.

"Take your mind off it," said Karen. "It'll come when you least expect it."

"That's what the inspector says." Nick shook himself into reality. "Where are we going?"

"I told you. We'll start our day again."

On this bright August day, the city of Salebourne was lovely. They walked, hand in hand, through the Cathedral and its close, and along by the river. They stopped at a riverside pub and had sandwiches and a Diet Coke on the benches outside. But Nick could not forget the morning. Besides, he had a nagging feeling deep down that he should not be here, for all to see, with another girl. The one everybody thought he was paired off with – even if it seemed that perhaps he wasn't after all – was dead. But as the day wore on, he didn't care. They walked, talked, about horses, about each other, then – with no crying but with quiet affection – Margie.

Karen liked him. He knew it – even though there had been that time when...

They sat on a bench by the river. Dusk was starting to fall: soon the Cathedral floodlights would be on. He looked at Karen while he thought she was unaware. Yes, the short brown hair, clear green eyes, were unlike Margie; Karen was utterly different, in looks and – he knew – personality. She was calm and steady where Margie had been emotional, impulsive. Margie had excited him so he was on the edge and over the top; Karen calmed him so he could face this terrible day. She alone had kept him together.

And she hadn't mentioned her being a jockey once.

He sat quiet in the gathering darkness. Was she waiting for something? For him?

The trouble with girls was, you *never* knew what they were thinking.

But Nick knew what *he* was thinking. This day had changed him. Nothing could be the same again.

Karen sat still, looking straight ahead.

It was the moment.

Or was it? He had an impulse to throw his arm round her shoulders, kiss her. He knew her face would turn towards his. And it did. But then they drew apart, knowing it would be an insult to someone dear to both of them. They sat together, quiet, thinking.

Nick still shook, breathed fast. He knew that another day, he and Karen would...

Karen took his hand again.

"Let's go now, Nick," she said.

As they came home on the last bus, Nick felt they were on the way to becoming a well-established couple. When he finally let himself into the Fanshaw's guest house, he was more content than he could have thought possible. With Margie it had always been difficult. He knew full well that everybody within a five-mile radius fancied her rotten. She knew as well; every moment with her was a trial for him. He knew she'd go, she'd laugh at him, he'd lose her: someone bigger, richer, older would take her away – and in the end had.

He would never have that feeling with Karen. He knew he'd always be comfortable with her. Even so, he suddenly wanted to cry his heart out in his room. He slipped in through the front door and started to dash upstairs.

Too late. A downstairs door opened. The other stable-lads were in the sitting room, playing cards.

"Come on in, Nick," shouted Jimmy Linnell and pulled him in.

Well, they were his mates. He couldn't just ignore them. He prepared to tell them about his momentous day.

But they didn't seem interested. They had their own news.

"Strange things happened today," said Ray Ling, the oldest there. "Sir Norbury Greyling turned up in his Roller this morning. Disappears with Johnny, then Alf sets us working like idiots to make things perfect for him. Greyling comes out, wanting to see everything, especially Mornington Sunrise. It makes you wonder if something's going on. Especially when a new stable-lad appears from nowhere this afternoon."

"Well, they *say* he's a stable-lad," said Kenny Birch. "But stable-lads don't start here in their forties. Not unless they're after Alf's job."

"And they don't have an empty flat over the stables

cleaned out especially for them in two hours," said Jimmy.

"And Alf's not behind the door in telling new lads what to do. He looks scared stiff of this one," said Kenny.

"So does Johnny," said Ray. "Not Connie, though. She looks like she fancies him."

"Connie?" said Nick. "Fancying a stable-lad?"

"This one looks more like he's in the SAS," said Jimmy. "There's something strange going on. Margie, Greyling in his Roller, this new man…"

"You don't think Sir Norbury had Margie got rid of, do you?" said Kenny. "Had she been off with the rich and famous and got to be an embarrassment? Scope for blackmail there."

"I wouldn't put it past her," said Jimmy. Then, seeing Nick's face, "Sorry mate. Don't listen to me. It's just been such a funny old day."

"Watch it, you!" said Ray, sudden anger in his face.

Nick saw his chance. He managed to rush upstairs before the others could pin him down. Once inside his bedroom, he locked the doors, threw himself on the bed and let go all the strain, all the trial of the long hours since he found the horror on the Downs in the early sunshine.

5

The house-to-house enquiries yielded useful information. People in the houses opposite had seen little out of the ordinary. Two remembered Ted Firs' recently-bought Ford Capri, a car so showy that many knew it better than they knew him, being driven to the end of the road and parked outside the house. One watcher was sure the person who got out, locked it up and disappeared round the side as if going in through the back door was Ted. The other wouldn't swear to it. The policewoman who saw the first asked if it wasn't strange that he didn't go in through the front door. "Everyone keeps front doors locked and uses back doors in Carver Street," was the answer.

Those opposite, sleeping in back bedrooms in both Carver Street and the next road down, Doone Street, saw drunks in the back alley. Several agreed on the time – about half-past two. They watched them stagger all the way up the alley, then all the way back. "They must have come up the wrong one," said a man in Doone Street. "If they'd made a noise I'd have been out there."

"Weren't they singing or shouting?" asked the constable. "Drunks usually do."

"Funny, that," was the reply. "They were dead quiet. More like sleepwalking."

"So how did you know they were drunk?"

"Because they staggered. One of them had to be propped up like he was out for the count."

"And two came up and two came down again?"

"Yes."

The barmen and bouncers at the Zero Club all remembered Margie and Ted. They were regulars. Margie had been seen with Ted a few times recently. Yes, they knew all about Ted. Seldom seen once upon a time, and then so scruffy he nearly didn't qualify to be let in at all. Once in, because he wasn't very bright, he had to have an eye kept on him. But what a change lately! Ted had transformed himself. Yes, they had a few flash types in there, some really had got something to flaunt. But, overnight, Ted started out-flaunting them all.

"He said he'd come up on the horses," said a barman.

"Must have been in a big way," said the constable, in the deserted, darkened bar to the sound of vacuum cleaners.

"You're right," said the barman. "The last couple of nights our Margie was all over him."

"Do you know Nick Welsh?"

"The little jockey? Of course. He's in here sometimes. Keeps off the booze, though."

"Has he been here with Margie?"

"Quite a lot. He was obviously crazy about her. I wondered what would happen when he saw her with Ted."

"And what did happen?"

"Welsh came in with his mates from the stables. He saw them together, looked like he'd seen a ghost, went off on his own straight away."

"You don't know where?"

"No idea. If they're not shoving money over the bar I'm not interested."

"What time was that?"

"About ten. His mates didn't stay long after he'd gone."

"What time did Firs and Margie leave?"

"I'm not sure. It got very busy about ten-thirty. I saw them dancing about eleven. By eleven-thirty I'm sure they weren't in. But I didn't see them go."

The bouncers confirmed. Nick left about ten and walked towards the bus station on his own. The friends he'd come with left very soon after but went towards a pub. Margie and Ted had left at about eleven-twenty, closely followed by two men they didn't know who'd come as guests.

"Whose?"

"No idea. Too many we don't know get in here saying they're someone's guest. Sometimes, when they see them, the members are too scared to say otherwise."

"Which way did they go?"

"All of them to the car park."

Inspector Chase was pleased by all this.

"So we've got a good scenario of what might have happened," he said to his whole team at Matley. "Margie's in the Zero Club with Firs, her new meal ticket. Nick Welsh sees her, rushes off crying his eyes out like he said. An hour and a quarter later, Margie and Ted leave, closely followed by some unidentified visitors."

"They may have nothing to do with it," said Ruggles.

"True. It's most important we find out who they were. Three hours later, Ted's Capri is driven back home. Whoever was driving it – and we're pretty sure it wasn't Firs, even though the driver wanted any watching insomniacs to think it was – goes round the back of the house and waits for his friend to come, probably carrying poor old dead Ted by the shoulders so he looks like a paralytic drunk being brought back home. Our new arrival slips the bolt on the back gate for them, they dump Ted in his own back garden, leaving him so – as they think – he won't be discovered until his mum comes back, then stagger back so it looks like they've made the sozzled mistake of going up the wrong alley. Now, what do we get from that?"

Ruggles spoke. "That Margie and Ted were killed together at about one o'clock in a place which is within at the very most one hour's driving distance away. Probably a lot less."

"Right," said Chase. "This is forming up nicely. Now what about Nick after he left the Zero?"

"I questioned the drivers at the bus depot," said a WPC. "The driver of the ten-fifteen bus out of Salebourne remembers him. Says he looked dreadful. Like he'd had a real shock. Nick was a regular passenger, often with Margie, and there aren't ever many getting on at the terminus at night."

"So Nick, it seems, is in the clear," said Chase. "I'm glad of that. Now, anything else?"

"Yes," said the constable who had questioned the barman at the Zero. "There's something odd which may or may not have anything to do with this. The barman told me that a rumour built up in the club that night which was all over the place by the end. Everybody's convinced there's going to be some sort of trouble next week at Buckingham Races."

"What sort of trouble?"

"No idea. But the rumour seemed to come from nowhere and was all over the place by closing time. The barman hadn't heard it before. And clubs like that are good places to keep your ears open for things you wouldn't hear otherwise. Is it relevant?"

"I don't know," said Inspector Chase. "But it makes you think. Yes, it makes you think very much indeed."

* * *

Mrs Fanshaw was used to getting up at five in the morning to make breakfast for her lodgers before they went to the stables. Nick was among them that morning, well over his trials of the previous day but still distraught about Margie and looking forward to a good gallop on Mornington Sunrise to blow it all away. So he was furious to find that he was not to ride the star horse.

"The new man's on him," grunted Alf.

"Why?" Nick's voice was a howl of disappointment.

"Guv'nor's orders," was all Alf would answer.

Nick watched this new man as he walked all round Mornington Sunrise, peering at him as if examining a diamond for the tiniest of flaws, looking into his eyes, his mouth.

"He looks more like the vet than a lad like us," muttered Nick.

The new man checked saddle, girths, lengthened the stirrups – he was taller and heavier than anyone-else there – and then swung himself easily up. Nick watched, puzzled.

Nick was fobbed off with Chucklehead, a roan mare belonging to Billy Boney. She had won a couple of races at minor meetings but was nowhere near Mornington Sunrise's class. The moment she put one hoof in front of the other, Nick would feel it.

"Am I being punished?" he said to Alf. "What happened on yesterday's gallop wasn't my fault."

"Don't worry," said Alf. "You'll be back."

As they walked out of the stables towards the Downs, Nick stole another look at the new arrival. He rode easily, like an expert. But not, Nick felt, like a jockey. Under his helmet was a square, grim face. He did not share in the talk as the horses first walked, then trotted, then cantered to the gallop.

"What's his name?" muttered Nick to Kenny on Sheikh Naseem's Mirage Oasis.

"Drake," Kenny replied.

"What's that, then? His first name? A nickname?"

Only the owners referred to them all by surname. For anyone, Connie and Johnny downwards, to call a working colleague by surname would be unheard of.

"Alf said we'd got to call him *Mr* Drake," said Kenny. "Well, blow that. Johnny and Alf may work us half to death but at least they're matey with it."

Nick agreed. At Arthur Kiteley's stables, he'd heard from lads in the pubs, you were expected to know your place; surnames for the lads, "Mr" for the head lad and "Sir" for Kiteley himself. And they didn't seem very happy.

The day was overcast, unlike yesterday's glorious sunshine. The horses thundered across the bare Downs and across the chalk track where yesterday Nick had made his awful discovery. His heart beat fast as they passed the spot. Police still scouring the area stopped to watch them go. Then back again. Chucklehead moved well underneath him. She was a pretty good mare. But he sighed for Mornington

Sunrise's brilliance. He guessed the difference must be that between an Escort and a Mercedes.

Drake did not extend Mornington Sunrise. Perhaps, thought Nick, he couldn't. When they were back in the stables, rubbing the horses down, getting their feed, making all well for them, Nick looked again at Drake. Mornington Sunrise was still in his care alone.

And odd thought entered Nick's mind. *This is a time of upheaval and calamity. Has his strange arrival anything to do with the murders?* Then an even stranger thought. *The murders came the first time I rode Mornington Sunrise. The new man comes and suddenly I'm not riding him. Has all this anything to do with Mornington Sunrise? He may be brilliant, but after all, he's only a horse.*

He took his eyes away from the hard-working Drake. *Of course not. That's just fantasy. What can the deaths of the saddler's daughter and a half-baked twerp have to do with the best horse on the flat in the country?*

"Rumours. I hate them," said Ruggles.

"I find it very interesting," said Chase. "We're always being called to sort out trouble in the Zero Club, yet that Saturday night seems the most sedate for years, even with two murders off-stage. The most memorable thing seems to be everyone talking about the races."

They had questioned as many as they could trace who were in the club that Saturday night. Yes, there were a few in who weren't regulars. Of course people came in from miles around who'd never been there before. Oh yes, there were often a few punch-ups inside and fights outside. The police should know *that* well enough by now. *But not that Saturday night?* Oh no, very quiet. *The newcomers?* No, they were very quiet as well. Just talked, drank – not very much – and listened. *Listened?* Oh, yes. *Who to?* Anyone and everyone. Now you come to mention it, it's like they'd just come to hear what was going on. *Did they talk to you?* A bit. Said they were down from London for a few days. *Did they ask questions?* Not much. *Were they separate or together?* Now you come to mention it, though they came at different times and stayed separate, you got the feeling they were together. Weird, that. Must have been my imagination. *Did you see either of them talking to Margie and Ted?* No more than to anyone else. *What did they look like?* One tall, thin, ordinary. The other had thick fair hair and beard. *A wig? False beard?* Could have been.

So the questioning went on, until Chase had a very definite view of a band of newcomers coming in simply to "get the buzz".

"What do we know about the Zero?" Chase asked Kemp.

"Not very posh, to say the least. The up-market places are on the other side of the city, near the river. The top racing people keep to the hotels in Matley. But a lot of stable-lads and their girlfriends use the Zero, along with the hard men of Salebourne and their birds. Most fights are between Salebourne and Matley people. As most of the Matley crew are eight-stone jockeys, the fights tend to be one-sided. I often wonder why they still go."

"So if someone wanted to get a low-down on the latest in the racing world, the Zero might be a good place to be?"

"Perhaps," said Kemp. "The odd drunk stable-lad might tell you something interesting."

"If I wanted a hot tip," said Ruggles, "I wouldn't go to the Zero."

"So what's with this rumour?" Chase said. "What trouble will there be at Buckingham Races?"

The questioning had tried to find out.

Did you hear about this business at Buckingham next week? Oh, yes. Everyone was talking about it. *What's supposed to be going to happen? A doping scandal, a terrorist bomb?* Could be. I've no idea. It's just that something big's going to happen, it will make all the headlines and it will break at Buckingham. *Who told you?* I can't remember really. *Was it Ted Firs?* I don't know. *Was it one of the strangers?* Definitely not. Everyone was talking about it except them. They just listened. *Had you heard it before?* No. *Would you be interested if you had?* Not really. I don't bother much about racing. *Are you interested now?* Of course I am. I want to know what's going to happen.

"Funny that Welsh said nothing about the rumour," said Kemp.

"He had more on his mind," said Chase. "The

whole thing sounds to me like someone shouting his mouth off, making something out of nothing, just to look big."

"Ted Firs?" said Kemp.

"Could be."

"Is this rumour connected with the murders?"

"Could be. I hope not."

"Why?"

"I told you. I want these murders to be a jealous lover getting his revenge: we find him, put him in the nick, end of story."

"But it's not, is it?"

"Sadly, no. This is the tip of something big. I've got a nasty feeling we'll end up dealing with some very important people indeed."

A WPC called to Chase.

"Sir. Phone for you. Urgent."

Chase took it. He listened. His face tensed. Kemp watched, suddenly sure of what was to come.

"Where?" Chase snapped into the phone. Then, "Right. We're on our way."

He put the phone down.

"Another murder," he said. "This one's nasty."

6

The morning passed for Nick with the usual round of work while the horses were given their freedom on the extensive grass round about. He watched Drake work. The man never spoke but got on with his tasks. He was experienced and efficient, there was no doubt about that.

But why should so old and able a person come here as a mere stable-lad when most were taken on at sixteen after a nine-week course at the Racing School at Newmarket? Why, the man was – unworthy, impossible, disloyal thought – as good at his job as Alf Simpkins was.

At mid-morning his thoughts were interrupted. Alf called him.

"Nick, Johnny wants you in his office."

Nick seldom found himself invited upstairs. This must be something big. What could it be?

Oh, no, not the sack. He might have brought the stables bad publicity. He'd been, however briefly, a double murder suspect. Lads had got the boot for far less.

"Go straight in, Nick," said Beryl.

He entered. Johnny stood there, with Connie. Connie, the power behind the throne, some said. Next to her husband, with similar short yellow hair and (he had to admit) a similarly red face, she looked more like a twin than a wife.

He's too scared to sack me on his own, was Nick's first thought.

Then he looked again. They were smiling.

"How are things, Nick?" said Connie.

"Not bad," said Nick guardedly.

"Have you got over yesterday's shocks?" asked Johnny. "Bad business. I know how upset you were."

"I'm better now."

"I'm glad," said Connie. "Well, Nick, we've got news for you."

"Yes, Nick, we have," said Johnny.

Nick waited. Here it came.

"I'm going to give you three rides at Buckingham."

Nick's heart lifted. He couldn't believe it. He thought he'd blown his chances of any at all.

"Thank you, sir," he stuttered. His gratitude was such that "sir" was the only word he could use. Dazed, he turned to go.

"Don't you want to know what they are?" said Connie.

"Oh, yes," said Nick. Almost an afterthought: the big news was that he was still in favour.

"Chucklehead in the 2 o'clock," said Johnny.

Billy Boney's horse. He knew from this morning that she wasn't bad.

"Mirage Oasis in the 2.45."

Sheikh Naseem's pride and joy. Better and better. Johnny wasn't giving him rubbish.

"And here's the third, Nick. Mornington Sunrise in the 3.30. The big race of the day. The Gawcott Stakes."

Nick had to sit down. This was amazing. This was like winning the pools, the Lottery and a date with Pamela Anderson all at once. He was not yet eighteen and he was being put on the greatest horse since Shergar in a big race. Unbelievable.

He stared at the smiling Connie and Johnny. "Thanks" was all he could stammer.

"You're good. We believe in you," said Connie.

"Don't let us down," said Johnny.

Nick almost shook with happiness. So much so that he had what he could afterwards only call some sort of brainstorm. But then, he felt good about himself, Connie, Johnny, the world – and Karen. Perhaps this was the moment. So he pushed his luck.

Johnny wouldn't do for this. He spoke to Connie.

"Mrs Rumbold–Straight, can I ask you something?"

"Go on, Nick."

"It's about Karen Thorpe."

Every trainer for miles around knew Karen's ambitions.

"I'm tired of being pestered by that girl," Johnny growled. "I run an all-male stables here. I'm not bringing trouble in."

"Times change, Johnny," said Connie. To Nick, she said, "Tell her to come and see me. We'll work something out." She turned to Johnny. "Why not send her to Newmarket on a course?"

Nick went out, very pleased with himself and only slightly worried that he might have annoyed Johnny.

An angler on the River Sale, about six miles east of Salebourne, had found the body. The river wound reedily through a gently-sloped valley overlooked by Matley Downs. Here it was close to the road and about a mile from the junction with the road to Matley. He had fished at his usual place all day with no luck. So, mid-afternoon, he walked two hundred metres along the bank and set himself up again. Then he saw a black plastic bag in the reeds. He stretched across to pull it out, hating needless pollution of his fishing waters. A white, dead hand appeared, dangling from inside the bag.

Chase and the team were there twenty minutes after getting the call. The find was gruesome. The body was of a man in his thirties or forties. He wore only vest and underpants. He had been shot in the back of the neck. But what appalled Chase most as the body was laid carefully on the bank was that it seemed someone had deliberately bludgeoned the face to make it unrecognizable.

Dr Gregson soon reported to Chase.

"Dead about twenty-four hours," he said. "In the river for about the same time."

"Right," said Chase. "The body seems to have fetched up in the reeds. We need the river warden to tell us about currents to find out where it might have been put in. We've got to find out who the poor chap is as well. That's not going to be easy."

"Someone didn't want us to know," said Ruggles.

"I hate this," said Chase. "Things are out of control."

Nick came off work at six. He rushed back to Mrs Fanshaw's to clean himself up and change, then he went to meet Karen. He ignored the derision of his mates. But Ray Ling's open hostility was a different matter. "You're disgusting, going off with another bird and Margie not even in her grave."

Ray was a bit previous here. It wasn't like that – not yet. But why shouldn't he see Karen? Margie would have understood. Nick looked away and said nothing.

They were to go to Salebourne again, have something to eat, then to the pictures. McDonald's was all their purses could run to. Over a quarter-pounder and french fries, knowing Johnny would have a fit if he were to see what he was happily chomping, Nick dropped his big news.

"Connie wants to see you about being a jockey. She says she can get you on the course at Newmarket and take it from there."

Nick had looked forward to saying this from the moment he had left Johnny's office. It might set a seal on their relationship. *She helped me, now I can help her and reap the reward for months.*

But it wasn't like that. Karen didn't throw her arms round him in gratitude. Instead, she looked embarrassed, turned her head away and mumbled, "I don't know. I'll think about it."

"But it's what you wanted," Nick burst out.

"I've got a new job, in the kids' riding stable."

It was no use. Women are beyond understanding, Nick thought, and hoped the evening wouldn't be a waste of time as well.

It wasn't. Far from it. And after all, he reasoned as he walked her back at nearly midnight to her parents' house, if she's changed her mind, she's changed her mind. Nothing to do with me.

The river warden was helpful. The current would have taken anything fairly heavy downstream, not quickly, because the Sale was slow-flowing here. If an object were in the water about twenty-four hours, it was probably thrown in about *here*.

He pointed to a spot on the large-scale map on the wall of the incident room. Here, river and main road were very close.

"Anything else, you know where to find me," said

the warden, and went about his business.

"That's where we'll concentrate the search," said Chase.

Nick was home late. He was glad Ray was not around when he came back to the house. He slept well. His last thoughts before closing his eyes, besides Karen, were concentrated on one topic. How would he get to Buckingham for the races? Some years would pass before he surged there in a Mercedes like champion jockeys drove. And he couldn't go with Alf and Mornington Sunrise as usual because Alf said Drake was to go with him and Ray, and there was nothing he could do about it.

Drake was getting on Nick's nerves – and everybody else's. He moved around the stables like a spy. The theories spread.

"He looks straight out of the SAS," said Jimmy Linnell.

"Perhaps he's MI5," said Kenny Birch.

"Don't be daft. What would they want here?" said Ray. "More likely from the Jockey Club. Perhaps they're after some doping plot."

"Then I hope they've sent someone to every stables," said Jimmy. "This one's clean as a whistle."

They all watched Drake with deepening suspicion.

"Hard as nails," said Jimmy. "You can tell just looking at him."

Nobody had the courage to ask him.

Nick was going to Buckingham just as a jockey: he had no duties attending to the horses. So he had no particular right to hitch a lift on the hired nine-horse transporter. And Johnny saw his attendance on time in the right place as his own responsibility; Nick knew there was no reason to expect help from the guv'nor. But Alf obviously felt bad about not taking Nick with him.

"I'll have to go round to the transport firm," he said. "I'll have a word with the nine-horse transporter driver."

The spot the warden pointed out soon swarmed with the same team which had already picked over the Downs and Carver Street. There was a layby on the road here: tyre tracks in the grass showed something had reversed and driven off again. There were still signs of a heavy object being dragged across a stile and off the footpath through meadow grass to the bank. Broken reeds showed where a body could have been shoved in.

"Well?" said Chase.

"Looks like we've got their tracks," said Kemp. "Goodyear tyres, like those fitted to thousands of cars and vans. Not much to be learnt except that if it's the same people behind all three deaths, they've got a passion for scattering bodies all over the countryside. But who can say that they are the same?"

Chase decided that he could. He would build his theories up from that assumption and try to see a pattern. He needed some connection between this body and the other two. He drove back to the incident room, his mind swirling with questions. When he arrived, a fax was waiting for him.

Two people in the Zero Club the night of the double murder had evidently been thinking and had gone to Salebourne police station to pass on the fruits of their thoughts. Chase read the copy of their statement and set up an extra question to join the rest.

We were in the Zero Club the night of the murder and when we were questioned before we said how everybody was buzzing with a rumour about something big happening at Buckingham Races next week. It was silly because no one knew what it was and people were making up theories like it was a terrorist bomb or a big doping scandal. Since then we have been thinking and we remember who told us it to start with. It was Ted Firs. He was with Margie and they were drinking together and laughing and we spoke to them because we knew them both. We were surprised Margie was going with him. Ted was a bit full of himself because it wasn't too often that anything good happened to him and he was letting on like he had some big secret. He was tapping the side of his nose like he knew things nobody else did and said, "There'll be a sensation at Buckingham. Don't put any money on Mornington Sunrise." We didn't take any notice because Ted didn't work in a stables so he couldn't have any inside knowledge and we thought he was just trying to be clever. We thought he said "sensation" because it made him feel big, not because he meant it. It was only afterwards that people started talking about a bomb or doping. We didn't tell you this about Ted when you spoke to us because we had forgotten. But the rumour definitely came from Ted Firs first and Margie didn't try to shut him up like girls do when their boyfriends are being stupid.

Signed:
John Craig, 36 Southlands, Salebourne
Sharon Barker, 2 Church Close, Salebourne

Chase read it twice. Did it mean anything? If this wildfire rumour started with the dead man shouting his mouth off, was he trying to be big, so the rumour, like so many, was baseless? Or was he genuinely in possession of knowledge which a wiser person would have kept to himself? And could it have been a reason for his murder?

The team had been through all the details they could find of Ted Firs' trivial dole and odd-job life. They found nothing of any seeming possible interest. But there was something Chase knew he *had* to find out. Firs was a changed man in appearance, from scruffy sparrow to peacock overnight. He had bought an old Capri in exceptionally good condition (completely clean inside; Forensic had scoured it for clues) which didn't mean he was rich but did show he had received far more money recently than was usual for him.

It was very important that Chase found out where from. Yes, the fax had been important. The new body in the river had nearly driven thoughts of Margie and Ted out of his mind. Now there was another lead of sorts and a question to answer that he should have sorted out at the very start.

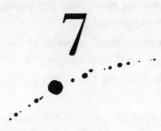

7

The Buckingham meeting started the following Thursday. All Nick's rides were on the Saturday; he would travel up early in the morning. But first there was something he had to do.

The police had released the bodies of Margie and Ted. On Wednesday, Margie's funeral would take place in Matley Parish Church. Nick had got time off to go to it.

Karen gave him a warning. "Don't stand anywhere near me."

"Why?" Surely Karen wasn't ditching him already?

"It's Mr and Mrs Moxon. They know we're going around together. They're furious. Mr Moxon called me a scavenger, picking up the scraps Margie left so soon after she was dead. And you should hear what he calls you. And his wife's worse. There could be a real scene if we don't watch it."

Nick was silent. He could see why.

"They think you must have done it," Karen went on.

Nick had got on well with Margie's father, a big, bluff, no-nonsense man, and her mother, sharp and blonde like her daughter.

"I can't believe that," he said.

"You'll have to," said Karen. "I didn't just leave the shop. He gave me the sack. Then she threw me out."

Nick considered this. "They can't do that," he said.

"Oh, can't they?" said Karen.

Nick could only see one thing. "Why can't you see Connie?"

Karen looked unsure again. "But I've got a new job, Nick. How can I leave it straight away?"

But there's more to it than that, he thought.

"What's the new man like?" said Johnny to Alf on the morning of Margie's funeral. They stood together watching Drake lead Mornington Sunrise out of his stable.

"He's a weird devil. Doesn't talk, doesn't want people to talk to him. I don't like it. I want my lads to be happy together. There's no room for bad feeling. It rubs off on the horses."

"You're a crusty old curmudgeon yourself with them sometimes," said Johnny.

"Ah, but they know me. They trust me," Alf

replied. "This new one, I wouldn't trust him further than I could throw him. Can I ask a question, sir?"

"I've told you all I can already, but fire away."

"Don't you think it's strange that a man like Greyling employs evil-looking characters like Drake?"

"How do you think Greyling got where he is? Not by employing St Peter lookalikes." Johnny checked himself quickly. "Anyway, I'm saying nothing. So you say nothing as well."

"That'll be hard. Everyone's muttering about him. And I don't fancy driving all over the country with Mornington Sunrise and only him and Ray for company."

"Sorry, Alf. But that's how it has to be."

Alf looked at him stiffly. Then, before he walked away, he said, "I think I get the message."

Yes, I think you do, thought Johnny. A feeling of disturbance, foreboding, swept over him. "The stench of danger is here," Sir Norbury had said. Johnny had no idea what it could be, but in his heart, after all that had happened recently – two murders affecting an employee, a third, sinisterly, of an unknown man but, everyone was sure, connected with the other two – Johnny knew Sir Norbury was right.

He'd heard this peculiar rumour about things in store to happen at Buckingham. He didn't believe it. Pub, club chatter. He knew what racing talk to believe and what not to. He always kept his ear to the ground. Things you could take seriously came from jockeys, bookies, other trainers – sometimes, just by looking at the horses themselves. From his usual sources, there was *nothing*. No, that smell of danger didn't come from Buckingham next week. He was *always* right about such things. Wasn't he?

Nick did as he was told. He kept away from Karen at Margie's funeral. They both stayed well clear of Mr and Mrs Moxon. Nick watched the large man and his still-slim wife stand mute at the graveside of their only daughter and felt shame for his conduct over the last few days. He had hardly allowed himself a moment to grieve. He had felt a lot for Margie: she had filled his thoughts and his dreams, yet as soon as he saw Karen that fateful morning, he had been off on a wild adventure the meaning of which he still wasn't sure about. No, it wasn't right. No wonder they'd sacked Karen. No wonder they avoided looking at him.

He watched Karen from afar. Yes, he really *did* like her. And she had obviously fancied him for … well, a long time, even after he had – oh, he couldn't help but recall it. He'd been at the cans of lager with his mates a bit too much, he knew that now. It wasn't just weight worries which kept him to the Diet Coke these days. And he'd swayed off into the village, met Karen and she was smiling to meet him and he'd opened his big mouth too much… Well, enough to say that he hadn't felt very good about himself next morning, was sure Karen would tell Margie at the shop, was convinced Karen would think they were boyfriend and girlfriend from now on. And that Margie would as well and just not bother with him.

But no, she couldn't have told Margie. And she didn't stop following him. And he never knew whether that flattered or irritated him. The shame came again when he realized that it had taken Margie's murder to show him which.

Nick recognized Inspector Chase and a WPC from the morning Ted's body was found. They stood apart, looking carefully at the mourners, showing respect but also watchfulness in case anybody interesting or unexpected turned up. But Nick could have told them – only family and friends were there. He knew the lot.

After the funeral, family and close friends had gone with the Moxons back to the flat over the shop. Inspector Chase had nodded to Nick, then left with the WPC. Nick and Karen, not invited back, stayed where they were.

At last they could come together. Karen had been crying. Nick tried to get her out of her sadness.

"Cheer up," he said. "Why don't you go and see Connie?"

"Give me time, Nick," Karen answered. "I've got to think."

He could have kicked himself. This really was the worst time to say such things.

It was maddening. Ted Firs had no bank account;

any money he had come by was in cash. And a fairly large amount of it. The car dealer he had bought the Capri from ("It was clean, that car. A really good motor.") reported a wad of old twenty-pound notes a month before. The only shop in Salebourne selling such exotica as men's leather trousers remembered Ted well – again it had been a month before and the same tale of a wad of well-used notes.

"Money for services rendered," Chase said to Kemp. "But what services, and who to?"

"And what do we make of Ted Firs telling someone who was no more than an acquaintance about Buckingham?" said Kemp. "Was that where the rumour started?"

"You mean Ted Firs trying to sound big?"

"Yes. But did he really know anything? After all, he's got no form. He seems to have been too thick to get into trouble."

"Is what he did or didn't know anything to do with the money?"

"And did the money come from the real source of the rumour?"

Suddenly, Kemp and Chase looked at each other, hope dawning.

"Have we got something at last?" Chase said. "Have we got a sequence of events? Firs performs some service for – perhaps was on the payroll of – some unspecified group of people who may have something to do with racing..."

"Something *crooked* to do with racing, because

they're planning some scam for Buckingham," said Kemp.

"And Ted Firs, with his little bit of dangerous knowledge, starts shouting his mouth off," said Chase.

They were silent for a moment.

At last Chase spoke again.

"We couldn't surely have found a motive for the murders? Ted knew too much, couldn't be trusted simply because he was fivepence short of a pound, so neither could Margie, because she was with him, so they both had to go. How's that for a theory?"

"Not bad," said Kemp. "Though it means we're up against very unpleasant people. But why litter the bodies everywhere so anyone can find them?"

"Correction. So *one person* could find them."

"Master Nick again," said Kemp. "He keeps coming up. And who were the two strangers in the Zero Club?"

"Well, you heard the bouncers and barmen. It's supposed to be members and guests only but they don't seem to know who they're letting in half the time. We'd better ask our uniformed colleagues to take a close look at the Zero Club when this is all over."

"Yes. But that doesn't help us much," said Kemp.

"You're right. The unknown visitors hold the key." Chase thought for a moment. Then: "How's this for an idea? Firs has got in with some bent outfit. It doesn't matter what for the moment. But they are *ruthless*. He's been paid cash for whatever he's done for them, seeming to suggest that was the finish with them for Ted Firs – 'thanks, here's your money, now get out' – and he feels on top of the world, really in the swim of things at last. Our mystery men gather in the Zero Club, what for I have no idea, and hear our foolish Ted open his mouth too wide. We have a good idea the night's rumour started with him. So he's hustled out and disposed of, to shut him up, because he's supremely expendable. Sadly for Margie, she's with him and has to go the same way."

Kemp thought. "Extremely nasty," he said. "And it's all to do with racing and horses."

"Right. And did Nick Welsh find both bodies through monstrous coincidence or was he meant to?"

"And if so, why?"

"And is the third murder anything to do with it?"

"It has to be. Coincidence doesn't stretch that far."

"So why don't we know who the third victim is? Why have his features been obliterated so deliberately?"

"There's only one reason," said Chase. "He mustn't, at any cost, be recognized. If he was, the whole conspiracy – because that's what it must be – would fall to the ground."

Kemp pondered for a moment. "It's all speculation," he eventually said. "All pie in the sky."

"We have to find out who the third victim is. And we have to alert our Thames Valley colleagues that there might be trouble at Buckingham. The racing authorities must be told as well. We've nothing else to go on."

"At least it's something," said Kemp.

For a brief moment, Drake gave up his monopoly on Mornington Sunrise. Nick was in the saddle again, on the practice gallop, feeling the marvellous responsiveness and intelligence of what he was sure was the greatest horse he would ever ride. But Drake was never far away, watching him, watching the horse, like a sinister nanny. As Nick trotted, Drake, on a chestnut filly owned by the Duke of Rothley, trotted beside. As Nick cantered, so did Drake. When Nick spurred Mornington Sunrise on with that smooth acceleration which he thought must be like driving a superbly-tuned Formula 1 racing car, he knew that struggling behind but never out of sight was Drake on the second-rate horse.

So his sheer delight in this wondrous beast was ruined. Drake made it seem like being a spoilt child jealous of Nick's sweets and toys. The single thought filled Nick's mind: *why is this man bugging me and everyone else as well?* Alf was no help. He either didn't notice or wasn't telling.

If the latter, then some secret was being kept. And with all that had happened lately, it wasn't long before another nasty thought came. *Is this secret about me? Am I not trusted? Is something terrible going to happen to me as well?*

Nick slowed Mornington Sunrise: the horse came

to a halt smoothly, with ripples of co-ordinated muscle. Alf was there, helping him off, and then unsaddling Mornington Sunrise and putting a blanket over him. Nearby, Drake swung himself off, unsaddled the filly and also flung a blanket over her back.

"Alf, Drake's really getting on my nerves. Who *is* he?"

"Just a stable-lad," Alf muttered, not looking at him.

Alf, Nick thought, you're a great man and a good boss. But you're a dead rotten liar.

Nick was unsettled. He felt he was being followed round the stables, watched as he went about his duties, everything he said judged as if there were hidden, ugly meanings in it. Only when he was with Karen did he feel comfortable, relaxed.

"I'm getting paranoid," he said to her that night.

"Shhh," she said, laying a finger on his lips. "Everything's all right. You've got me."

8

Buckingham Racecourse was in open country to the south of the town. It was a small course, popular with trainers, jockeys and the public. Good horses competed there. The star race of the meeting was the Gawcott Stakes, on the last day. It would be the biggest race on the best horse so far in Nick's short career as a jockey.

The course was a sharp right-hander, meaning that the horses ran round the main circuit clockwise. There was a slight downhill stretch after the start, some undulations, then a long level stretch before an uphill slog to the finish. This was punishing for horses tired after all that had gone before; many a race was won or lost over the last few furlongs.

Still, thought Nick before racing started, as he paced the course through, noting the firm going and each dip and rise, every course is different and I've got to learn the unique features of each one, as well as the individual characters of every horse I ride.

The day was fine. The car parks were filling up. The helicopters of the richest owners were landing and no doubt picnics were being unpacked and expensive meals were being prepared in hospitality suites and private boxes. Suddenly, Nick, on his own and purely happy for the first time in days, felt a shiver of delight and anticipation.

"*This* is my life, *this* is what I was born for," he said aloud. "I don't care how many times I'm thrown and trampled on, how many bones I break, I was made to race great horses and nothing's going to get in the way of that."

He'd better get back. The first race, in which he was riding Chucklehead, was two hours away. He should get to the changing rooms and don Billy Boney's racing colours, ready for weighing in.

Johnny had only entered horses for the first and last days of the meeting. On day one, Paddy O'Keefe had ridden his last three horses for Johnny. An ignominious seventh, a second when he should have walked it and a lucky third did not please jockey, trainer or owners. The next day, Johnny's complaining voice was heard all over the stables.

"What's the matter with Paddy? He should have walked the three o'clock."

Connie made sure everybody heard her answer. "O'Keefe's washed up. It's Nick you've got to look to now. He'll be your next main stable jockey."

"Good on you," muttered Jimmy Linnell to him. "If Connie wants something round here, it's as good as happened already."

"Well, I'm not paying Paddy a retainer for his services any more." Johnny's answer rang through the courtyard. "He's riding for Kiteley on Saturday. There'll be head-to-heads between him and Nick. That should prove something."

Nick looked at Drake to see his reaction to all this. As if he knew, Drake turned round. The face was expressionless, like a mask. There was no knowing what lay behind those dark, inscrutable eyes.

Chucklehead and Mirage Oasis, along with all the other horses racing (except Mornington Sunrise), had been led on to the big nine-horse transporter hired to take them to Buckingham that morning. Their attendants, Jimmy and Ken among them, were on board as well. Nick had no attendant's duties, but he had after all managed to hitch a lift in the cab with Len Roach, the driver. All the older jockeys would drive from their own houses.

It was all very well, but Nick missed going with Alf in Mornington Sunrise's single, luxurious box. Although Johnny didn't like it – indeed, had expressly forbidden it – Alf wasn't above stopping for a quick bite and a rest at motorway services on longer journeys. Nick was happy about this; he and Ray took turns to go while the other looked after the box and the horse. *I bet Drake won't let you stop*, Nick thought. Then: *Why not? Alf's the boss.*

Yes, Alf was. But Nick was sure Drake called the shots. Why?

The sixty-mile journey to Buckingham had been uneventful. Nick had had plenty of time for his walk round the course. When he came back he looked at his horses. Chucklehead and Mirage Oasis showed no signs of distress from their short journeys; they looked fit and raring to go. Jimmy and Ken were as well, thankful that this meeting had not meant a journey up the day before and a broken night with their charges in strange stables.

Mornington Sunrise was just as content. Alf, Ray and Drake, however, were tight-lipped. Nick guessed Alf had not enjoyed his unbroken journey.

But who cared? The atmosphere of a race meeting still had the power to excite Nick, so that what other people were feeling just faded away. The filling grandstands, crowds in the enclosure and along by the wide green course lined with white posts curving away into the distance, the colour, the chatter, bookies with their stalls shouting the odds – they all thrilled him beyond words. *Even if I never rode a winner in my life*, he thought, *this is what it's all about*.

But then, he *had* ridden winners: novices and selling platers at Southwell and Chester. So he knew what it was like four times already to be greeted by owner and trainer and led to the winners' enclosure. And he wanted it again. Today? Today he was on *class* horses. And if the magnificent Mornington Sunrise could propel him round the track to make it in the Gawcott, then he really would have arrived and the world at large, not just Connie and Johnny, would think he was pretty good. And so would Karen.

He allowed himself just a split second to think how Margie might have felt. Then he squashed it out of his mind.

The Thames Valley police had been alerted about possible trouble. Chase was surprised when the local detective-inspector told him that no whisper had come their way of anything out of the ordinary.

"You know as well as I do," he had said to Chase, "there's always somebody to grass or start a whisper. But there's nothing. Any trouble will be from outside, nothing to do with our local villains."

But there was a greater than usual police presence on the course and plain-clothes detectives mingled with the crowd. Chase, Kemp and Ruggles were among them.

Nick was ready for the weighing-in. His boots, breeches, helmet and Billy Boney's weirdly kaleido-scopic purple, yellow and mauve colours were on. The clash of the scales and the highly-charged voices all round were making adrenalin run fast through his body.

He knew many other jockeys already, well enough

to exchange greetings and wishes of good luck. Paddy O'Keefe, riding today for Arthur Kiteley, did not speak to Nick. His thin, weatherbeaten, sardonic face looked hostile. Nick had a sudden flash of insight: *deep down, he's afraid of me*.

Outside, Jimmy waited patiently by Chucklehead. Johnny was there as well, with an oddly lanky figure, famous on millions of televisions screens – Billy Boney. Nick expected quick one-liners. But no – instead, he leant up against the flanks of his horse as if he could not bear to let her leave him. *He's scared stiff*, thought Nick. *More scared than me*.

"Remember," Johnny was saying. "There's no need to let her rip. Play a waiting game. Too many leaders who look like they've got the race sewn up blow up on the rise in the run-in. You've got to keep something back for that. It's a killer."

"OK, Johnny," said Nick. "I've got that."

"I know you have," said Johnny.

Billy Boney stuck out his hand.

"Good luck, lad," he said. "Do your best."

Nick looked at the famous comedian, saw pleading in his eyes. *This means everything to him*, he thought.

Chucklehead was getting restive. It was time to get into the saddle. Now Johnny held her, Billy was prevailed upon to leave her side, Jimmy gave Nick a leg up – and there he was, the very picture of a jockey. He suddenly knew he was part of a long, unwavering tradition, from Dettori, Carson, Piggott, right back to Steve Donoghue and Fred Archer, and a century or more before even them. He could be on a faded print hanging on an ancient wall and look exactly the same.

"I've put a couple of quid on Chucklehead at 6 to 1," said Ruggles.

"I'm not sure if there's anything in the rules of police conduct about placing bets on horses ridden by murder suspects," Chase murmured.

Like many horses, Chucklehead did not like the starting stalls. Nick had trouble guiding her in and Jimmy had to cling hard to her halter to keep her facing the right way. Things weren't helped for any of the field of fourteen when Paddy O'Keefe's highly-strung mount, Raisin Cookie, nearly bolted. Jimmy, watching as he clung to Chucklehead, gasped, "Kiteley won't like that."

But at last they were all in the stalls – and suddenly the way ahead was clear and they were running.

Nick did as he was told. He knew Chucklehead had it in her to win this race if he rode wisely. He tucked Chucklehead in easily, lying sixth round the first turn. Now he was single-minded, knowing only the pounding body of the animal underneath him, the expensive horse-flesh all round him, the drumming of hooves on the firm going, the shouts of jockeys to their mounts and sometimes to each other, the wind rushing past his head as he concentrated on his own horse while he scanned the horses in front and his brain envisaged the horses behind.

Chucklehead was not tiring. *You beauty*, he thought. *You're better than they think*. Keeping to the outside, he began to move up the field. O'Keefe on Raisin Cookie was close ahead. Four furlongs out he made his move. He was in the lead. Chucklehead moved second. With some surprise, Nick realized the bookie's favourite was nowhere.

Now they were in the final straight. Only dimly was Nick aware of the yelling crowds by the rails. The slope upwards began; he felt it in Chucklehead's stride. Raisin Cookie was two lengths clear. Had Chucklehead got enough left? He urged her on, gave the lightest touch with the whip. And she responded. One length, half a length: a furlong to go. They were level. He was still on the outside. He was going to make it. He would have a winner.

But O'Keefe had got something extra out of Raisin Cookie as well. And suddenly Nick realized – *we aren't going straight for the winning post*. Raisin Cookie was actually veering towards him. They would collide, his left boot would tangle with O'Keefe's right; there would be disaster.

Instinctively he checked.

And Raisin Cookie was away, safely, winner by half a length.

Nick was shaking with anger as he dismounted. "You've got to object," he shrieked at Johnny. "That was dangerous riding."

"Cool it," said Johnny. "There was no bumping and boring. He was yards away from you. Nobody says you've got to run in a straight line to the winning post. O'Keefe's been at this game for years. You haven't. If you hadn't checked, you'd have won and O'Keefe would still have been nowhere near you. He banked on your inexperience and got away with it."

Nick felt completely deflated. "Sorry, Guv'nor," he said.

Johnny laughed. "Don't worry, Nick. Put it down to experience. You did better than I expected."

Nick was thankful. He had expected a rollicking. And Billy Boney was beside himself with delight at Chucklehead's second place. He wrung Nick's hand as if he were a ten-length winner, now he pushed his face into Chucklehead's neck and crooned, "We're on the way, my little darling." For a moment, Nick felt the content of being part of a well-pleased group.

This was shattered at once. Paddy O'Keefe, with Raisin Cookie's owner, a stable-lad and a man who walked stiffly, ramrod-straight, with bristling moustache and fierce expression, walked past to the winners' enclosure.

"Bested you again, then, Straight?" said the man. "Owners will soon see for themselves who looks after their interests." His voice was harsh, unfriendly, his look hostile.

Johnny was goaded into answer. "Get off, Kiteley," he shouted contemptuously. "Enjoy your little victory while you can. You'll be pushed into the shade before the day's out."

"You'd better work fast while you still have a licence," was Kiteley's parting shot.

Johnny's face turned dark red with rage. If Nick, Ken and Jimmy hadn't held him back he might have run after Kiteley and started a fight.

"Cheat," Connie yelled after him.

"What did he mean?" Johnny spluttered as he shook himself free. "He doesn't say things for nothing. *What did he mean about losing my licence?*"

Down by the rails near the winning post, Chase, Kemp and Ruggles had no idea about that little scene. Ruggles was philosophical about Nick not winning. Chase was patient.

"No trouble, no disturbance, nothing out of the ordinary at all. No stewards' inquiries, no buzz about doping – it seems like a wasted journey so far."

"How can a day at the races be a wasted journey?" said Kemp.

"No more bets for me in the next races," said Ruggles. "I'll wait for Mornington Sunrise."

A sudden idea crossed Chase's mind. "Yes," he said. "So will I."

9

Nick was unhappy after his next race. Mirage Oasis did not run well. Lying third coming into the finishing straight, he found the final burst to the winning post was beyond the horse. For all Nick's urging, there was no response, no surge. River Winkle close at his heels passed him, overtook the two leaders on the outside, and scored exactly the sort of victory Nick had planned.

"Don't take it to heart," said Johnny. "If the horse hasn't got it, you can't put it there."

"I should have run a different race," said Nick. "I should have been leading up the straight and tried to hold on."

"See? You're learning," said Johnny. He had calmed down after the spat with Kiteley. They had not even looked at each other, let alone spoken, since. But later, as he was putting on Sir Norbury

Greyling's colours for the Gawcott Stakes, Nick risked a word with Paddy O'Keefe next to him.

"What did your boss mean about Johnny losing his training licence?"

"How should I know?" O'Keefe, not unfriendly, grunted. "I only ride for him."

"Oh, come on," said Nick. "You must have picked something up."

"Put it down to the fact that they hate each other. If one found a way of putting something over on the other, he would."

Nick had to be content with that.

Mornington Sunrise was drawn on the inside for the start, which Nick did not like. He feared being boxed in early on as horses made for the rails by the shortest route. There was a large field, attracted by big prize money, and Nick wished Mornington Sunrise wasn't quoted as 3 to 1 clear favourite. He was on a hiding to nothing and already things were against him.

His tension showed as Alf pushed him up on to the horse.

"You'll do all right," said Alf.

Connie and Johnny were quiet this time, Sir Norbury Greyling was with them. He patted Mornington Sunrise on his muscled hindquarters, looked coldly at Nick, then seemed to soften slightly.

"Do your best, Welsh," he said. "I expect no less."

Nick felt even more apprehensive.

"I've risked a fiver on Mornington Sunrise," said Ruggles.

"I've a feeling you might lose your money," said Chase.

Nick knew the one to beat was the second favourite, Artificial Cream. And he knew who the trainer and jockey were. Kiteley and O'Keefe. Apart from anything else, he was racing for Johnny's pride.

Artificial Cream was drawn in the middle, where Nick would like to be. The horse was a beautiful grey, fourth in the Derby but improving all the time and already quoted as a likely bet for the St Leger. Interest was national in his contest with Mornington Sunrise.

Nick and O'Keefe did not speak to each other as their horses walked down to the start. Artificial Cream was excitable; O'Keefe was having some difficulty. Mornington Sunrise remained calm, unfazed by anything round him.

At last all the horses were in the starting stalls. Suddenly they were away. Mornington Sunrise set off fast – as if he was as worried about being boxed in as Nick was. By two furlongs the horse – as if he knew exactly what he was doing – had established a lead of a length. Nick soon ceased wondering if these were the right tactics; the horse underneath him was just different class.

Round the first bend, Nick kept Mornington Sunrise in the lead. He could imagine the bumping and boring going on behind him. He began to wonder if this might not be the easiest race he had ever run. Then he realized Artificial Cream was passing him on the outside. He saw O'Keefe crouched low, experienced and confident, and knew he had got a race on his hands.

"Why did you say that I might lose my money?" said Ruggles.

They could not yet see the race from where they stood but could hear the race commentary and knew there were only two horses in it.

"Just something that crossed my mind," Chase replied. "Forget it. It was stupid."

Nick was sure they were clear of the field. What did he know of Artificial Cream? Did he have the strength, speed and wonderful acceleration of Mornington Sunrise? Could he afford to let Sunrise tuck in now and risk everything on a final power-house surge up the slope? Or had the wily O'Keefe guessed that was what he would do and knew Artificial Cream had the power to hold him off? O'Keefe wouldn't go into the lead so early if he didn't know what he was doing. And besides, O'Keefe had psyched him out of one race today: had he got some unfathomable way of doing it again?

They were round the second bend. Still only two horses in it. If anything, Artificial Cream was increasing the lead. Nick couldn't let that happen.

Even Mornington Sunrise might be left with too much to do. He urged the horse on; he had to stay within two lengths. At the light touch of the whip, Mornington Sunrise smoothly increased speed. But, though Nick excitedly urged him on, the horse stayed fixed just a length behind, galloping almost in perfect step with Artificial Cream.

An amazing thought crossed Nick's mind. Was Mornington Sunrise reading the race better than he was? Daringly, he withdrew the whip. Perhaps Sunrise might make a move in his own time.

Another thought. *You're the jockey. You can't let the horse make the decisions. You'll lose, Johnny will half-kill you and Sir Norbury Greyling will destroy your career.*

In front of him were Artificial Cream's grey, plunging hindquarters and Paddy O'Keefe's back. For too long, it seemed as though they were all he would see. Beyond was the finishing straight, like a wide green tunnel, stands and crowds either side. From here, that final slope looked like a forbidding mountain. Two furlongs to go. One furlong.

And then he felt it. Like a rocket, a turbocharger, the smooth surge of power took him easily, naturally, with it. Mornington Sunrise, with no prompting, had opened up. They drew level with Artificial Cream; Nick saw Paddy O'Keefe's surprised, furious glance and saw he was using the whip on the grey horse – uselessly, for nothing could stop Mornington Sunrise now. With Nick almost a passenger, he passed the winning post two lengths clear.

Nick Welsh had won the biggest race of his short career.

"Well, I'm not down on the day," said Ruggles, counting his winnings.

"Is that all we came for, to make sure you weren't out of pocket?" said Kemp disgustedly.

"The day isn't over yet," said Chase.

Johnny couldn't help shouting at Kiteley. "Which stable's got the class, then?"

Kiteley angrily turned away. He was shouting at Paddy O'Keefe.

Nick dismounted. Mornington Sunrise stood calmly while everyone fussed round him. Johnny spoke delightedly to Nick.

"Brilliantly judged race," he said. "Run like a champion."

Nick said, "Thank you," and wished Karen was there.

Sir Norbury Greyling spoke as well. "I was surprised, not to say angry, when Rumbold-Straight told me he was entrusting my horse to an apprentice. But I should have trusted his judgement. First-rate show. You'll go a long way."

Nick basked in the compliments. But he had to confide about the race to somebody. After weighing-out and the presentation of the cheque and big silver cup by Lord Gawcott, great-grandson of the race's founder, he managed a word with Alf.

Drake was seeing to Mornington Sunrise. Nick felt surprise that he was nowhere to be seen before and after Mornington Sunrise's race. But that didn't matter. Alf was standing by the cab of the horsebox.

"Well done, lad," Alf said.

"But Alf, it wasn't me. It was the horse. I'd have made my challenge for the front a furlong before. But he wouldn't go. It's as if he said, 'I know what's best for me. I'll be the judge.' And then, coming up the slope, he just *went*. As if he'd worked it out for himself. He won the race, not me."

Alf listened. Then he said, "I could see that from the start."

Nick stared. "What do you mean?"

"I knew this horse was a genius the moment he came to us as a yearling. Something about him. He's quite capable of making his own decisions. He should win everything he's entered for."

"So why didn't he win the 2000 Guineas and the Derby?"

"Who rode him?"

"Paddy O'Keefe."

"Say no more."

"But Paddy's a brilliant jockey."

"Maybe so. He makes good horses look terrific and so-so horses good. But he'll never do well on the really top animals. He can't believe there are times when you just leave it to the horse. *He* lost the Guineas and the Derby, not Mornington Sunrise."

Nick was silent. Alf looked at him.

"You'll be a better jockey than he ever was, son," he said. "You're not afraid to give credit to a horse to know what he's doing."

"Not after today," said Nick.

Five o'clock. All the Matley horses were in their transports, the journey south started. From the passenger seat in the big nine-horse vehicle, Nick saw Mornington Sunrise's single box, Alf and Drake in the cab, set off in front. Len Roach beside him kept them in sight all the way home.

There was a police debriefing after the meeting's close. Chase, Kemp and Ruggles, facing a rebellious roomful of Thames Valley police whose leave had been stopped for nothing, were apologetic.

"Our information was wrong," Chase said. "What can we say but sorry?"

"Let's get out of here," muttered Kemp.

Matley was reached by seven. The horses were back in their stables, the lads, Nick among them, Alf and the still taciturn Drake had seen to their every need. Afterwards, Nick managed another word with Alf.

"I can't get over Sunrise. There *can't* be another like him."

"Depends what you mean by 'like'," Alf replied.

"What do you mean?"

"He had an identical twin. There could have been two Mornington Sunrises."

"That's no big deal. Lots of mares have two foals at a time."

"This foal was completely identical. No one could tell them apart. Not often that happens. Mornington Noonday, he was called."

"What's this *Mornington* business?"

"On the stud farm, they say, the owner had come for the birth. He, the vet and the stable-lads sat up all night waiting for the dam to foal. To while away the time, they played that daft game about tube stations. 'Mornington Crescent', it's called. Anyway, she foaled at sunrise and our Sunrise came out first."

"Where's Noonday now?"

"Dead. Broke his leg in a fall, had to be shot. Tragic. That was just after Sir Norbury bought Sunrise at the Newmarket Sales."

"Would Noonday have been as good, do you think?"

"I don't know. Probably not. I can't believe Sunrise's sort of greatness touches more than one horse in a generation."

"But Noonday. A thoroughbred one-year-old shot," said Nick wonderingly.

"He'd be no use," said Alf. "He'd never race so he'd have no form so he'd be no good at stud. This is a hard game you're in."

"I know," said Nick. Of course there was no sentiment in racing, but he still hated to think of such things.

"Don't worry. It would have been properly done.

The vet would've been there, a humane killer used, Jockey Club informed."

"Where was this?"

"Very near here. At Kiteley's, eighteen months ago. Even I felt sorry for such a thing happening to him. Someone bought the horse at the same Bloodstock Sales as Greyling bought Sunrise. Kiteley trained his horses, so he took the risk, as all trainers do. Don't worry about the owners, though, or Kiteley. They're all well insured."

"That's not the point," said Nick.

"I know," sighed Alf. "But you can't afford to keep a horse who won't earn his living. Best get him in the catfood tins quickly."

Drake came out of Sunrise's stable, wiping his hands. He said nothing, but plainly all was finished.

"Let's go," said Alf.

They went their separate ways, Nick feeling slightly sick.

Kemp drove on the journey back. "Good day out, waste of time," he said.

Chase didn't answer. He was lost in thought.

"So we were spun a yarn," Kemp went on. "They were all having us on. No big sensation at Buckingham."

Chase continued to watch the unfolding road silently. At last he spoke.

"That, I think, was the big sensation."

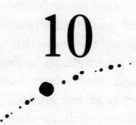

10

After Nick had said goodbye to Len Roach outside Mrs Fanshaw's, he let himself in, went up to his room and sprawled on the bed. He needed a good wind-down after such a day and before meeting Karen.

He let his mind wander into nothingness. The sensations were too close, too amazing to sort out. All he knew was that he felt *huge* satisfaction. He had arrived at the top, *early*. Could he stay there?

Well, he'd pleased two owners today at least. Billy Boney, for whom horses seemed to be everything, even more than his own career. Would Billy have rather been a jockey after all? Nick tried to imagine the lanky beanpole sitting on a horse. The thought made him laugh out loud. Well, good, that's what Billy was for, to make people laugh out loud.

And Sir Norbury. There was no doubt that before

that day Nick had been scared stiff of the very idea of seeing Sir Norbury. But today – well, no matter that those were patronizing words he'd used. "*First-rate show. You'll go a long way.*" They were like music to his ears.

What a weird game racing was. That two such different people were so important to him together, so bound up in it, so well able to share the same joy, the same triumph. Sir Norbury wasn't in it just for the money. He could buy and sell racehorses like potatoes. And Billy – well, he was *besotted*.

Nick tried to imagine the two standing together. It was possible – they had only missed each other by a few minutes. What a contrast they would make. Chalk and cheese. In his mind they stood next to each other, praising him. His eyes closed. Before he drifted off to sleep, they seemed to merge into one figure standing, watching him.

And suddenly he sat bolt upright. Was this an illusion? They had merged – *into the same person*. A stern, powerful face, a loose, hangdog clown's face – they were superimposed on each other *and were the same*.

No, they weren't. *You're tired, mate*, Nick thought. *You need half an hour's kip.*

He lay back, closed his eyes and drifted into sleep. But not before a little voice at the back of his mind had said, "They're *the same*. What does it mean?"

When he woke refreshed an hour later he had forgotten all about it.

* * *

Connie and Johnny drove home in the Range Rover. They were well pleased. They had won a major race for their biggest client, seen their best horse run to something like his full potential and discovered – not that they didn't know already – that they had a really great jockey for the future.

And, probably best of all, Johnny had put one over on Kiteley.

"He didn't like that," he chortled. "Which stable's got the class? That took the smile off his face."

Connie merely murmured, "Yes." The rivalry between the two stables – and more importantly, the two trainers – had lasted too long for her to think of it as anything but an unquestioned fact of life. She looked back to the roots of the hatred between her husband and Kiteley. There was so much behind it. Sometimes she wondered if the main cause was herself. After all, she had been friendly with Kiteley before this fresh-faced young man had come along with his great plans and had fascinated her so much that they were married before she knew quite what had happened. Kiteley took this quietly but, she knew, deeply. Then there was the time of the great doping inquiry twenty years back, when Kiteley had been up in front of the Jockey Club and had as near as a whisker lost everything and been warned off racing for ever. Johnny had nothing to do with getting him there. But Kiteley believed he had – anonymous letters, secret telephone calls, baseless accusations. Kiteley had vowed revenge, publicly, one dreadful evening in the Feathers in Matley. Johnny protested his innocence, but there were plenty to hear that night and since then the village had tended to split into two camps, as well as the stables. Why, it had even crossed Connie's mind that these murders were something to do with the endless confrontation. But Kiteley would never go as far as *murder*, would he? Of course not.

It went even without thinking about it that neither would Johnny.

"Oh, Johnny," Connie had once said. "Let's call a halt to all this. Life's too short. Call a truce. Let bygones be bygones."

"I hate the twerp," Johnny had replied. "And if you're married to me, so should you."

A pity there had been no chance to stay in Buckingham for a celebratory meal at the White Hart and a get-together with other racing folk. But time was money. Their place was back in the stables. They'd have a meal in the Feathers in Matley instead.

"You should have come to Buckingham," said Nick to Karen. They were having their usual Diet Cokes in a Matley pub. "You could have, now Mr Moxon's given you the sack."

"I watched you on Channel 4," she replied.

Karen seemed rather distant tonight. Nick had hoped for no-holds-barred admiration. Fat chance.

"If you took up Connie's offer, you could be riding

winners yourself in a year," he said. Surely that would get a response.

She turned her glass round on the table, studying it as if it held some secret. "Maybe," she said.

What a dead loss.

"What did you mean, that *was* the big sensation?" said Kemp, when they arrived back in Salebourne.

"Do you believe that a hundred people in a club one night are all going at once to take the police for a ride?" said Chase.

"They'd love it," said Ruggles.

"But it's unlikely, I admit," said Kemp.

"I'm sure now that was a genuine rumour, passed on in good faith. I think Ted Firs did start it, but he was sure he knew his stuff. He dropped hints in his daft pub-talk which were real and Margie didn't stop him. And I'm not just speculating now, I'm ninety-nine per cent sure that's why he was killed."

"Ted expendable *and* a liability, you mean?" said Kemp. "And poor Margie just got in the way?"

"Perhaps. But maybe she was deeper in it than that."

"But there's nothing we've found out about Firs that connects him to anything or anyone suspicious."

"He got all that money. Don't forget that. We haven't *half* done our job on Firs' background. Or Margie's."

"I'll set them all looking again," said Kemp, taking the hint.

Once again, Nick was walking back on his own after getting Karen to her parents' home and not enraging them too much about what time it was. He was very happy. Karen had loosened up a lot; everything was great, he realized, as long as he didn't push Connie's offer. This seemed an amazing turn-round for her – he pondered on why it was. The only answer he came up with was that she had already decided they were a couple: two jockeys together would be just too much. Well, if that was so, it made him feel even better – though he was still surprised.

Still – Karen and Mornington Sunrise. What a great double! Would he be riding Sunrise in the Puckeridge Cup at Bishop's Stortford next week? Would he carry on so he rode the horse up at Doncaster in the St Leger? Alf thought he should. What had he said about O'Keefe? "He makes good horses look terrific." But he would never get the very best out of the top horses. "He can't believe there are times when you just leave it to the horse." Well, Nick certainly knew that now. What a tonic Sunrise had given him. Johnny *had* to go on letting him ride the wonder horse.

He knew he would never sleep that night, his brain was too active and he was too happy. So he didn't walk straight back to Mrs Fanshaw's. He took a long detour out of the village, down narrow, hedgeless lanes towards Johnny's stables. He couldn't go in; once outside after work there was no re-entry.

Barbed wire, security cameras, prowling guard dogs, the lot. The total value of horse-flesh behind those fences ran into millions. Alf, as well as Connie and Johnny of course, and now Drake, actually lived on the site. There was always a duty stable-lad sleeping overnight in case of emergencies; Nick had escaped such chores now he was a regular jockey. Who was on duty tonight? Nick had no idea.

He passed the main gate. The night was warm and the new moon shone, outlining everything in ghostly grey. He looked through the gate towards the court-yard and the main stables. The courtyard, as always at night, was lit up. He could see the darkness of the stable doors against the whitewashed walls and the windows of the upper floor.

As he watched, a light went on in one of the windows. Who could be there? An intruder? No, the light must be from the flat the duty stable-lad used.

No. That window was on the other side of the courtyard. So who?

Of course. Drake's flat, the one that had been so quickly cleaned out. So the man of mystery was still up. Unable to sleep because still high over the day's events? Nick doubted it. He had hardly been seen during the day – not even before Mornington Sunrise raced, or after he had won and Johnny and Sir Norbury Greyling were smothering Nick with congratulations. That was odd, wasn't it? Johnny had given orders that Drake was to travel with Sunrise, be his attendant.

No matter. Drake was a law unto himself. Alf seemed to think the new man was almost taking the stables over, so it looked as if he could do what he liked.

He turned away and walked towards the village. The road was deserted, unlit. Nick, though, had no fears of muggers or thieves in this quiet place. Any lying in wait out here would waste a lot of time.

A quarter of a mile on – or two furlongs, as he preferred to think – just as he was entering the High Street, he heard a popping noise behind him: a little motor-bike. The rider passed him.

Nick knew who it was. Ray Ling on his Honda. Where could he have been? Johnny's stables was the only place along that road for three miles. And now Nick remembered who was on duty. It wasn't Ray: it was Kenny.

By the time Nick reached the house, Ray had taken his helmet and gloves off, propped the Honda on its stand and was just about to open the front door.

"Hi, Ray," Nick said. "You're out late. Where've you been?"

Ray looked at him. His voice could only be described as a snarl. "None of your flaming business."

Nick, taken aback, said nothing. Ray went on, "And I don't have to ask where *you've* been tonight. Filthy rat."

Nick found his voice. "That's none of your flaming business either."

He pushed his way past Ray and into the house.

"You still haven't said why no sensation might have *been* the sensation," said Kemp.

"Have you read Sherlock Holmes?" said Chase.

"Every word," Kemp replied. "But that was before I joined the force. Real detective work isn't like that."

"Oh, it can be," said Chase. "And in this case I think it might."

"I don't understand," said Kemp.

"Holmes got involved with racehorses as well," said Chase. "*The Silver Blaze*. Murder, and a horse faked. A case of ringing. And you'll remember what gave Holmes the vital clue?"

"Well, I must admit that just for the moment I seem to have forgotten," Kemp answered.

"It was the curious incident of the dog."

"What about the dog?"

"It didn't bark."

"Why should it?"

"Because guard dogs are meant to bark at suspicious intruders. There was supposed to be an intruder – but the dog didn't bark. So Holmes deduced that nobody had broken in during the night and the villain was someone the dog knew. The dog didn't bark when he should have, so Holmes solved the mystery."

"Are you telling me, that because there was no great sensation when you thought there would be, you've solved the mystery?"

"I wish I could. But I'm convinced now that we

know why Ted and Margie were murdered. I'm certain our third unknown victim was intimately connected with the whole sorry business and that whatever was supposed to happen at Buckingham will have been postponed to another meeting."

"Which one? There's racing all over the country all the time."

"Well, let's have a bit of deduction here. We're in Matley, so it's a meeting where horses from Matley stables are running…"

"That could be anywhere as well. There are other stables here, as well as Rumbold-Straight's and Kiteley's," Kemp interrupted.

"…and purely because the one person most affected by the murders so far works for Rumbold-Straight, it's a meeting to which Rumbold-Straight's horses are going."

"I can easily find that out," said Kemp.

"In fact, I'll go further. It's a meeting at which our Nick Welsh will be riding. It's inevitable. Everything seems to revolve round him. We can never keep him out of it."

"OK," said Kemp. "So we find out where it is. You've convinced me, but it's still only speculation. Is it enough to get leave stopped for another poor lot of policemen? I should think your name's mud round Buckingham now."

"Probably," said Chase. "I'm not bothered. But you're right. We can't expect more co-operation."

Kemp was already on the phone. He was speaking

to Beryl Lackland. "Thanks," he said and put the phone down. He turned to Chase. "Bishop's Stortford next week," he said.

"I wonder if we could manage a trip into Hertfordshire ourselves?" said Chase.

Nick was called into Johnny's office again that morning. More good news. But the meeting did not start well.

"Beryl tells me the police rang up asking when you're riding next."

"It's nothing to do with me," cried Nick in alarm. He could see his career evaporating before it had started.

"Ah, they make you sick. Don't worry about them," said Johnny. "I just want to tell you your mounts for next week. Three on the last day at Stortford."

Well, he knew he'd be riding. But O'Keefe would be back on Mornington Sunrise, so it was no big deal.

"Chucklehead again in the 2 o'clock."

OK. He and Chucklehead got on well. And he'd meet Billy Boney again. He was always pleased to see that extraordinary breath of fresh air.

"China Chimneys in the 2.45."

The Duke of Rothley's horse. A tall four-year-old chestnut. Not a bad horse, but no classic.

"And Mornington Sunrise in the Puckeridge Cup."

Nick stared in disbelief. "Does Sir Norbury Greyling know?"

"Sir Norbury saw you at Buckingham. He knows you get the best out of the horse."

"Sunrise gets the best out of himself," said Nick.

"You *let* him. Sign of a great jockey. Paddy has to impose his will whatever the circumstances." *That's what Alf said*, Nick thought. "Sir Norbury saw how you and Sunrise surged past Paddy. O'Keefe was on a good horse, but together they had no answer. Sir Norbury's convinced. O'Keefe will never ride Sunrise again. You will."

Nick now couldn't believe his ears.

"You mean at Doncaster in the St Leger?"

"And in France in the Arc de Triomphe. And in the US Breeders' Cup. I only wish you'd ridden him in the Guineas and Derby. He'd be known as the greatest horse of the century by now."

Nick felt quite faint. He had to sit down.

"Here, have a drink," said Johnny, reaching for the whisky.

"No, thanks," said Nick. "Except tonic water. I don't any more, you see."

Johnny laughed. "I like to see a jockey take his work seriously."

I'll never tell you the real reason I gave up, Nick thought.

Johnny went on. "But when you win the Leger I'll get the champagne down you."

Yes, you will, Nick thought. And I'll drink it too. In bucketfuls.

11

The week passed with no real developments. The list of Ted Firs' activities grew as Kemp stepped up the enquiries. He had picked up cash in hand over the years working on back-street car lots as a cowboy mechanic who could be a convenient fall-guy for the real cowboys when things went wrong, and also doing odd jobs at various stables round Matley: sweeping up, mucking out when even the regular lads turned their noses up. He had never, it seemed, been to Johnny's. But he had worked once or twice at Kiteley's.

"That piece of scum?" Kiteley had said when Ruggles had asked him about it. "But don't think I'm heartless. I'll help anyone down on his luck." His eyes narrowed. "You notice, of course, that Rumbold-Straight did not extend the same helping hand?"

Ruggles had noticed a lot – the gleaming stables, a cross between an army camp and an open prison, the downward twist of Kiteley's already stern mouth when he mentioned Johnny. No love lost there, he thought. Could this evident feud be significant?

"Poor little twerp. He never came round here. I'd have known. I'd have helped him," Johnny had said when asked.

A question occurred to Ruggles which, when he relayed it, Chase agreed was worth answering. Firs lived in Salebourne; Matley was six miles away. How did Firs get there so regularly? Bicycle? Bus? Hitch-hiking? In an old heap disowned even by the shady car dealers he sometimes worked for? However he travelled, he must have been a familiar sight in Matley. So how come Nick Welsh didn't know who he was?

"Well, I didn't, that's all," Nick said when Ruggles taxed him on it. "I didn't grow up in Matley. I only came here six months ago. That's why I live at Mrs Fanshaw's."

Ruggles was satisfied. Chase wondered, though, if Ted's sudden money could be explained because he saved what he earned from his casual jobs. So Ruggles went the rounds again.

The sums mentioned were pitiful. "I have no idea," Kiteley barked. "Ask Connors, my head lad. He deals with casual work."

Ruggles did. The money paid to Ted Firs at Kiteley's stables was even less than at the car lots.

Ruggles added up all the sums he was told of. Hardly enough to buy one of the Capri's alloy wheels.

Ruggles asked all the trainers whether Ted had done anything to warrant a big one-off payment. They all laughed. Kiteley asked him to leave the premises and promised a solicitor's letter at what he took to be an implied accusation. The car dealers' response involved neither solicitors or laughter but was just as final. Ruggles sometimes wondered why he had so wanted to join the CID.

Meanwhile, the team at the incident room had made enquiries by phone and fax, pored over mug-shots of known villains, scoured missing persons files, been out to draughty pubs to hear what snouts and grasses had to say. And as a result, the identity of the dead man in the reeds of the River Sale was no nearer discovery.

"He's got to be *somebody*," Chase roared in a rare moment when frustration got the better of him.

"It's a London gangland killing," said Kemp. "They've just dumped the body out a bit further now Epping Forest's full up and there's security guards round all the new road building sites watching for protesters. You know what they say about the foundations of the M25? Well, the villains' graveyard is just coming further out of town."

"The murders are connected," said Chase firmly. "I *know* it."

"Perhaps things will become clear at Bishop's Stortford?" said Kemp.

"They'd better," said Chase. "We're just thrashing round in the dark at the moment."

Bishop's Stortford was further away from Matley than Buckingham – along the M25 and up the M11. If Alf didn't have Drake with him, Nick knew he would give himself a break at the South Mimms services where the M25 met the A1. That's what he had done going to the spring meeting. Nick had been with him, on his very first visit to a racecourse as an employee of Johnny's. He had felt very apprehensive guarding a fortune in horse-flesh on his own in a packed lorry park, full, for all he knew, of potential horse-thieves, while Alf lingered inside over a cigarette, a sausage roll and a cup of coffee.

No chance this time, Nick thought. The workaholic Drake would keep him driving till he dropped.

As for Nick, he had made the same arrangements for getting to Bishop's Stortford as he had for Buckingham. He liked Len Roach. The fine summer weather was just on the turn as the meeting started. Once again, Nick was riding on the last day only; he knew Johnny regarded him as an apprentice still and would not expose him to the full rigours of the jockey's life. So, on the last day, under a cloudy sky and in a brisk wind which showed autumn was not far away, Nick one again paced the course before racing started.

The course was a left-hander: horses ran anti-clockwise. Bends were tight. Here, the upward slope came at the start – a steady rise for two and a half furlongs. Then came a long, fairly flat stretch until the last dip over the final furlong led to fast finishes. Nick needed to work out different ways of nursing his horses along from those at Buckingham. The two courses were like looking-glass reflections of each other.

The atmosphere as he approached the winning post and stands worked on him in just the same way, though. *I shall have a great day today*, he thought. *I feel it in my bones.*

At least he wasn't coming up against Paddy O'Keefe until the final race for the Puckeridge Cup. He saw him in the changing rooms, O'Keefe shot him a glance but did not speak. Other jockeys, though, were friendly; he was congratulated on his win in the Gawcott Stakes by some of them. He could see Paddy didn't like that. *So what?* he thought. *You make enemies on the turf as well as friends.*

Again, he slipped on Billy Boney's colours, put on the helmet, picked up his whip and went to the weighing-in. The adrenalin was once again coursing round his body; he wanted to be there, shooting out of the stalls, taking the lead...

No sooner had he reached the open air than a hand clamped over his shoulder and a familiar voice sounded close to his ear.

"Do your best today, lad. You and Chucklehead. Do your best."

It was Billy Boney. Nick turned to look at him. He

was shocked. The hangdog, lantern-jawed face which only had to twitch to send millions into helpless laughter had nothing funny about it today. Billy Boney got half his laughs out of playing the permanent depressive. From close up, Nick could see he was *really* depressed: his brown eyes were deep with sadness, his mouth creased with worry.

"Don't worry, Mr Boney," said Nick. "Chuckle-head's a good filly. We'll do all right, her and me. We nearly won last time, and this time there's no Paddy O'Keefe to get in the way."

"All power to you," said Billy Boney. "I know you'll do well." But his face did not split into the gap-tooth grin which caused even more waves of laughter across the nation.

Is it true what they say about the tragedy under the clown's mask? What's he got to be sad about? He's the most popular man in the country. So Nick thought as he stood by Chucklehead with Johnny and Jimmy Linnell already there.

"You're at 8 to 1," said Johnny. "That's a good price. A bet on Chucklehead's worth fifty quid of anyone's money."

Nick, with a leg-up from Jimmy, nimbly settled in the saddle. He looked at Billy standing there, thought of Johnny's last remark – and realized: Billy had met him on what could have been his way back from the bookie's ring. Had he put a lot more than £50 on Chucklehead? Was that the reason for the other side of Billy Boney that he had seen so briefly?

No time to think. Johnny was talking about the race ahead.

"Take her easy at the start here. It's no use having a three length lead at the first turn and then being so tired that the others just coast past you because they only cantered up the slope." Nick nodded. "Just keep up with the rest over the first two furlongs. Don't let them get ahead either. It's possible to have too much to do."

Nick dared a question. "What if she *wants* to go at the start?"

"Use your head. It depends on the horse. There's some who think this course is a doddle, others that it's a killer. Your horse will tell you which."

Chucklehead's got a big heart, thought Nick. And she's strong. I'll know what to do.

Now the walk to the start began. Chucklehead was quiet, only starting to fret when she saw the starting stalls ahead of her. But getting her in was easier than at Buckingham; she trusted Nick now. And when the gate flew up and the horses burst out, she wanted to go. She was in the lead at once. After a furlong, Nick risked a quick look back. He was already two, three lengths clear. The other horses were bunched, slow, taking it easy up the hill, ready for a long easy gallop afterwards. The sight reminded him of riders in a cycle sprint race, bunched, slow, waiting for one to make a break.

I've done it wrong. I'm tiring her out. They'll all pass me as Chucklehead tires, he thought. Then, *I know*

Chucklehead. She couldn't race like that. This horse has plenty left. She can win.

Now he was four lengths ahead. They were at the top of the rise. He knew the others would now try to open out.

Soon he heard them. His lead was cut. They were gaining. Their hooves were louder in his ears; he heard the jockeys shouting. Chucklehead heard as well. She responded to Nick's light touch with the whip. *She* wasn't going to be caught by that rabble.

Over the long level stretch she kept her lead. *Get to the dip at the end and we've won*, Nick thought. *And nobody can put us off like O'Keefe did last week.*

One horse was close, making a move. It was within two lengths of them. Nick didn't know which horse it was, only that it was threatening them. But Chucklehead knew as well. They were at the top of the dip, the winning post beckoned down what looked, foreshortened, a considerable hill. Chucklehead saw it too – a final invitation to shake her pursuers off. Down the hill she tore. Nick, elated, piloted her to the winning post under the stands, to the shouts of the crowd. Her only challenger had been left standing. They had won by three clear lengths.

Nick was almost delirious as he slowed, leaned forward, patted Chucklehead's neck and waited for Johnny and Jimmy to hold her before he dismounted.

"She's not just good, she's *brilliant*," he exulted. "She's different from Mornington Sunrise. She's a front runner. Put her in the lead and she's desperate to stay there."

"You took a big risk. I was worried," said Johnny.

"It wasn't a risk with her," Nick replied. "She loves it."

Billy Boney was actually capering round them. When Nick was back on the ground, he pumped his hand until it nearly dropped off. "Wonderful, wonderful, *wonderful*," he kept repeating. Then he seized Chucklehead by the neck and kissed her forehead. "You little *darling*," he cried.

Then he dashed off. Nick watched him go. "He didn't stay long," he said.

"Off to get his winnings," said Johnny. "You've probably saved him this afternoon."

"I don't believe it," said Nick. "He must be filthy rich. A millionaire. He's one of the top entertainers."

"Maybe so," said Johnny. "But he's obsessed with racing. He gambles big and loses. That's where it all goes."

Connie leaned towards Nick so no one else could hear. "I'll tell you a secret," she said. "Billy Boney is the one owner we have to chase for stable fees. He'll have put two grand on you today at least. That means we'll get paid on time and some arrears sorted out as well. I brought a bill with me just in case. I'll be at him the moment he comes back. You've helped us a lot today, Nick."

Billy returned, beaming. As promised, Connie went straight to him. The bill was settled before they reached the winners' enclosure.

Ruggles had put exactly one two-thousandth worth of Johnny's estimate of Billy's stake on Chucklehead. So he only wore a slight smile of satisfaction when he rejoined the others.

"This is *not* what we came for," Chase said sternly.

"Well, there's nothing else happening," said Kemp.

True. Once again, there was no sign of anything but an ordinary British race day like thousands of others. Every theory Chase had considered seemed about to fall to the ground.

"So why do I keep thinking, *wait for Mornington Sunrise?*" he said.

12

The next race was such a let down. China Chimneys never got going. Nick couldn't make him; they finished well down the field a dismal eighth. The Duke of Rothley just stalked off as if Nick was a sort of cockroach lucky not to be trodden on and never even commiserated with him.

But all would be better in the Puckeridge Cup. Alf stood by the familiar tall form of Mornington Sunrise, holding him by the head as Nick, wearing Sir Norbury Greyling's colours, vaulted lightly into the saddle. Sir Norbury stood with Connie and Johnny.

"Just make it a hat-trick," said Johnny. "Gawcott, Puckeridge and the St Leger. It will make up a bit for O'Keefe missing out on the Derby and Guineas."

"I will," said Nick confidently.

Sir Norbury said nothing, but in a rare outgoing

gesture, gave Mornington Sunrise a slap on the rump.

Then the horses started the long walk down to the start. Paddy O'Keefe was on Artificial Cream again. The grey horse stood out against the rest of the generally brown and chestnut field.

"Good luck. You're still learning, lad," he said good-naturedly as the two horses paced together.

"I won't let you cut me out today," Nick answered. He was still sore about Raisin Cookie at Buckingham.

"All in a day's work," O'Keefe replied. "No harm intended. You're new; you fell for it. You'll do worse yourself when I'm old, stiff and on the streets."

Nick looked at him sharply. He had assumed he was building up a sort of racing feud with Paddy, just as Johnny had with Kiteley. Obviously he was wrong. And he was pleased. Falling out so early with a fellow jockey seemed a terrible thing. He laughed.

"You, on the streets? Never. You'll be a top trainer yourself and I'll ride winners for you."

"You're on," said O'Keefe and raised Artificial Cream's speed to a canter.

Nick thought there was a slight edginess in Mornington Sunrise which he hadn't noticed before. In the stalls he was quiet enough, but constantly reached his head forward as if he had no idea what lay beyond. Odd behaviour for so experienced a horse.

They were under starter's orders. With the usual rushing rasp, the gates went up. The sixteen horses were away.

Straight away Nick knew Mornington Sunrise was far from his best. There would be a fight on today, both with the other horses, and with Sunrise himself. At the top of the rise after the start, they were lying seventh. Artificial Cream was two places ahead. This was about how Nick had seen things going; he should be pleased. Sunrise's extraordinary powers of smooth acceleration just when it was needed ought to carry him into the lead whenever Nick wanted. But Nick was worried. He wasn't getting that unmistakable feeling of awesome strength in reserve. If Sunrise were to win today, it would be through his good riding, and because all the other horses were just as much off form.

Once on the level, the field began to string out. The runners from the front were coming into their own. Now Artificial Cream took the lead. Nick brought Mornington Sunrise into fourth place and thought: *I should be starting a long run in behind Paddy now and Mornington Sunrise should take the race late like he did last week. He's far and away the classiest horse in the race.*

But today there was no unstoppable instinct for the winning post. For all his urging, Nick could get no answering burst from the horse. Round the last bend down the slope to the winning post, and he should be going like the wind and passing them all. Instead, it was Artificial Cream who had won and Mornington Sunrise struggled in a poor sixth.

He heard booing in the crowd. Many people would

have lost a lot of money. With a dull inevitability, he knew there would be trouble about this.

Alf and Johnny caught the horse by the head. "Get down, Nick," said Alf.

But Nick couldn't. He sat still, tears of disbelief and disappointment filling his eyes, unable to face Johnny and Sir Norbury.

"You can't stay up there for ever," said Alf.

Unwillingly, Nick dismounted.

"What in God's name went wrong there?" Johnny demanded.

"I couldn't help it. He'd got nothing to offer. He was like a different horse."

Sir Norbury Greyling was in a towering rage. "You deliberately held my horse back," he roared. "You lost the race on purpose. You had the field at your mercy in the back straight and you *chose* not to press your advantage. I'll find out whose orders you were under and I'll have your licence revoked, and both you and whoever you are working for warned off for life. Meanwhile, you'll never ride a horse of mine again." He turned to Johnny. "And as for you, if I find you are playing a dirty game, I'll ruin you, Rumbold-Straight."

He turned on his heel and strode off.

"It wasn't my fault," Nick stammered.

"There'll be big trouble now," Johnny groaned. "Once he's made other arrangements, he'll be taking his horses away from us. Just watch all the rest follow. And Greyling won't be the only one who'll think you pulled the race. There'll be a dope test of course and a stewards' inquiry for sure. Perhaps worse."

Indeed there was a stewards' inquiry. Nothing could alter the race's result, of course, but Sunrise's performance was such a gross reversal of form that the crowd seemed on the point of revolt. Nothing, though, could be found. Nick protested what he had said all along, that Mornington Sunrise had had nothing to give when called upon and he was as shocked as anyone. The horse had a dope test – the result was negative. All seemed as it should.

"Don't worry, Nick," said Connie, putting her arm round his shoulders in a motherly sort of way.

"You'll have to forget it. Put it down to experience. There's no use us falling out. We're all in this together." Johnny's voice was strained. Nick knew that underneath was real anger. And why not?

"I don't believe this," said Ruggles. "That's the surest five quid I've ever known gone down the pan."

"We came for a sensation again," said Kemp. "And all we got was the favourite off-colour in the big race of the day. Annoying for some but not exactly world-shattering."

Chase was silent. A thought was forming in his mind but he didn't know quite what it was. At last he spoke.

"I'm not so sure," he said. "Perhaps that *was* the sensation."

* * *

Drake was there with Alf by the single horsebox again as Nick climbed disconsolately into the transporter cab next to Len Roach. And once again the thought crossed Nick's mind: *why do I never see Drake actually at the track?* It was as if his duties to Mornington Sunrise ceased the moment Alf led him out of the box. Strange. Or was it all of a piece with his silence, his unapproachability?

And why, thought Nick, *am I bothering with him when my mind is full of its own misery?* Until this afternoon he had been the coming man; why, only that morning a newspaper had called him "the new young hope of British racing". Now what was he? A has-been at eighteen who couldn't guide a great horse through an ordinary field, who ignominiously lost on the red-hot favourite, who had been banned from riding the horses of about the most influential owner there was outside the Royal family? No use thinking *who cares? There are plenty of other owners.* Johnny was right: all the rest would follow. But riding horses was all he knew. It looked as though he was destined for a life scraping a living begging for rides, going from course to course sucking up to arrogant trainers and at best being fobbed off with hacks, selling platers, novices.

He saw nothing of the journey back to Matley: the M11, the M25, the motorway services which Alf in the single horsebox ignored because the stern Drake sat beside him. Because by now another set of worries was invading his mind. Johnny was saying nice things at the moment. But this *was* a hard game. Johnny and Connie would only be good to him while he was doing well. He had let them down. Johnny had gone out on a limb for him with Greyling, and he'd been made to look a fool, his judgement defective. Once they were home and had a good think, it would be, "On your bike, Nick, and bye-bye Matley."

And another thing. *What would Karen think?*

As the heavy diesel engine ate up the miles, Nick's head fell forward on his chest in complete misery.

Nick was right. Johnny's anger couldn't stay bottled up for long. "I'll drive home," Connie said, knowing the signs. He was wise enough to let her.

"I'll lose all my horses," he raved in the passenger seat. "I'll be known as the idiot who put an incompetent apprentice on a great horse and ruined it."

"But Johnny," said Connie. "Nick *is* a good rider. You think so, I think so. You can't damn a jockey on one race. He won brilliantly on Chucklehead. The fault can't be in him. It must be in the horse."

"How can it be? Mornington Sunrise is a *wonderful* horse in perfect nick. Losing the Derby and Guineas was bad enough – at least O'Keefe brought him home a good second. But Sunrise showed what he could do at Buckingham – now today he runs like a little girl's pony. The dope test was clear – they'll all say that if it wasn't the jockey holding him back then it's my training that's at fault. If it's the first, Nick's finished; if it's the second, I am."

At last he was quiet. Connie drew breath to speak. But he started again.

"Just a minute," he said. "If people think that Nick held the horse back, there'll be a full inquiry by the Jockey Club. Greyling will call for it, you can bet your life. They'll look at videos of the race, they'll make up their minds, and it's hell's own job trying to appeal. If they think Nick deliberately stopped Sunrise winning, they'll ban him and warn him off all racing. They'll try to say he ran to my orders and they'll look to see if I've made a fortune backing Artificial Cream. Well, I haven't, so that's all right. Even so, I could lose my licence."

Now Connie did manage a word. "That's nonsense, Johnny."

But Johnny ignored her. His face had gone rigid and red with anger.

"Just a minute," he roared. "What did Kiteley say last week? That I'd lose my licence? The *rat*. He *knows* something. *He's* behind all this. He's set it up."

"Rubbish," said Connie calmly. "How could he?"

"*Then why did he say it?*"

Connie didn't reply.

At least Chase, Kemp and Ruggles did not have to apologize to another police force this time. As Ruggles drove, Kemp asked Chase a question.

"You're talking in riddles again. Just because

Mornington Sunrise didn't win, why should you say that was the sensation?"

"I don't know yet," Chase replied. "I must sleep on it."

Nick had arranged to meet Karen as soon as he was free of the stables after returning from Bishop's Stortford. He nearly didn't go. But he pushed himself.

"Oh, Nick," she said. "I saw it on television."

"I don't want to talk about it," he replied. "You must think I'm rubbish."

But it seemed she did not. And as he walked back to Mrs Fanshaw's lodging house, Nick pondered on yet another mystery about her. When he was triumphant, she hardly seemed to bother. Now he had failed, it seemed – well, it seemed almost as if she were trying to make it all up to him. And he appreciated and enjoyed this process. But it also, in ways he could not understand and which were too deep for discovery, disturbed him. Nearly as much, in fact, as the obsession he was developing with these two owners. Billy, who cavorted round like a delighted puppy, and Sir Norbury Greyling, who threatened the end of his career. The light and the dark. Chalk and cheese. The mask of comedy, the mask of tragedy. Two sides of the same coin. How could they be anything else?

So why could he not stop his mind from seeing those two extraordinary faces merging into one?

13

Nick did not take a detour past the stables tonight – that was the last place he wanted to see. He walked straight back from Karen's – just in time to see Ray Ling on his Honda arrive from the other direction.

"At it again?" Ray said contemptuously. "You stink."

"None of your business," Nick grunted. Then, because he had always thought Ray was a friend, "Ray, why do you take what I do so seriously?"

Nick had already unlocked the front door. Ray pushed past him and started to stalk upstairs. After three steps, though, he stopped and turned round. His face was twisted with anger.

"I take nothing that you do seriously," he hissed. "What concerns me is what you *ought* to be doing and you're not. So I've got to try and do it for you."

"What do you mean, Ray?"

"Well, if you don't know, I'm sure I'm not going to tell you. You're either thick or nasty. Probably both. And what I've found out already would wipe that greasy smile off your face."

He turned again and disappeared upstairs. The slam of his door echoed through the house.

Nick entered his own room and sat on the bed. Another reason for the day to be such a bad one. Before, Nick hadn't bothered about Ray's anger with him. Now he was worried. All right, his sudden shift to Karen as soon as Margie was dead might not have been ideal – but life went on, you only live once and all that. Nobody else seemed to worry. So why should Ray? Poor, twenty-eight-year-old Ray, who'd never be a jockey with his gammy leg and who'd never amount to anything in the racing game. What was wrong with him? Jealousy?

Who of? Him and Margie? Or him and Karen? Had he fancied one or the other? Or both? Or neither, and this was all directed just at him alone?

Nick made a resolve. He'd have it all out with Ray next day.

That night, he dreamed – a long, complicated, disturbing dream. Margie visited him. She was very close and very real. One moment she was as she always seemed to him; the next, she was laughing at him, taunting him, calling him a fool for trusting her. Then, as he watched, she sprang on to a horse which he realized she had been leading towards him all the time, though he had not noticed it while she was laughing at him. She galloped away on it and he realized the horse was Mornington Sunrise. "Come back, that's my horse," he shouted, but it was no use because they were too far away – except that suddenly Margie was back beside him with no horse at all. And Karen stood with her and there were Kiteley, Paddy, Sir Norbury Greyling and Billy Boney there as well – and they all seemed angry with him. No, they were more than just angry, they were threatening, they were going to do him injury. And then he saw the dead bodies lined up: Margie's and Ted's and others he didn't know but knew he would if he could bring himself to go closer. And he knew, with a wrenching twist of the stomach which forced him thankfully awake, that he would join them very soon, unless...

The room was dark; outside was quiet. He sat up, put his reading lamp on, looked at his watch. Only half-past three. The fright of the dream had left just two faces hovering before him, staring, merging in front of his eyes. Billy, Sir Norbury. *Oh, stop that. What can those two have in common?* No, his mind was trying to deal with something difficult, concealed.

He lay there, trembling slightly. It was no use trying to sort this out rationally. He was mired in terrible events, racked with grief one moment, high on triumph the next.

But there had been something in that dream he'd just come out of, something that could be the key that, if he could find the right lock to turn it in, would let him open a door on to a new scene, where he could see it all hanging together. Margie, Karen, Ted Firs, Kiteley, Johnny, Billy, Sir Norbury, Drake, Alf – somewhere with them was the solution.

He switched the light off and lay in darkness waiting for sleep to come again. And suddenly he was sure – *the solution, he had just dreamed it*. He had not recognized it and now it had gone, slipped tantalizingly away like a blob of mercury.

He tried to trap it again – but now he was fully awake, could only think of yesterday's disaster in the Puckeridge Cup. "But I won on Chucklehead," he said aloud. No use; every moment of that terrible, powerless time came back – that dreadful ride on a horse that wouldn't respond, that just hadn't got it, that – and here he sat bolt upright with the force of what hammered through his head – WAS NOT MORNINGTON SUNRISE.

Inspector Chase had not slept well either. What had he meant in the car? Was it just daft or somehow profoundly true? If so, how? Mornington Sunrise had been beaten and he had said, "Perhaps that *was* the sensation."

By the time he had finished his breakfast, kissed his wife and got into the car, he thought he had at least enough to try out on Kemp before talking to the whole team. So, as soon as he could, he started.

"When you got home last night," he said, "what

did you think of our two trips to the races?"

"Good days out, waste of time," said Kemp. "The favourite being beaten is *not* a sensation."

"So perhaps you don't think this series of murders had anything directly to do with racing?"

"I didn't say that. But I think we're barking up the wrong tree."

"So Ted Firs' rumour in the Zero Club wasn't significant?"

"No. Just a hopeless wannabe trying to impress. It couldn't be why he was killed."

"Well, I disagree. I still think Ted Firs' indiscretions in the Zero Club are the most significant detail about the case so far."

"How, when it didn't come to anything?"

"Let's step back from it all," said Chase. "Look at the whole picture. On the one hand we have three murders. A young girl and her hopeless layabout boyfriend and someone who still, despite all our efforts, remains unidentified. On the other hand we have a huge horse-racing industry centred on the single village of Matley. What connects them?"

Kemp considered. "Ted Firs' rumour connects everything bar the third murder," he said.

"And?"

"I can't think of anything."

"What about Nick Welsh?"

"But we've discounted his connection as coincidence."

"I'm not so sure. He fits in somewhere. He

thought Margie was his girlfriend, he found both bodies. Anything else?"

"You tell me."

"The nearest thing to the sensation we were looking for was the unexpectedly poor running of the favourite in the big race of the day. Who was riding?"

"Nick Welsh, I suppose."

"You see? Isn't it amazing? Everything out of the ordinary seems to centre round that young man."

"But the favourite losing *wasn't* out of the ordinary," Kemp insisted. "The dope test was OK, the stewards' inquiry showed nothing, everyone's in the clear."

"When the favourite loses, so do a lot of other people. And a lot of others gain."

"We all know that. What's that got to do with it?"

"It seems a long time ago now that I said this had all the hallmarks of a conspiracy. I'm sure of it now."

"OK. But conspiracy to what?"

"That's what I can't fathom out. There's only one thing I can think of which would fit the bill properly."

"Yes?"

"Ringing."

"Meaning?"

"Secret substitution of one horse for another. It's been tried before, sometimes very successfully. Why, it's even part of the villainy in *The Silver Blaze*."

"What, the Sherlock Holmes story you were on about coming back from Buckingham?"

"The very same. I think that somehow another horse was substituted for Mornington Sunrise and ran in its place. The question is, will it happen again?"

"Why? So someone can win a few easy quid off the bookies?"

"No," said Chase thoughtfully. "Surely not just for that. There's something very much bigger behind this."

"Big enough for three murders?"

"If the stakes are high enough and the people at the top are ruthless enough, then human lives become expendable."

"So where does Nick Welsh fit in?"

"He rode Mornington Sunrise. But did he know if there was anything wrong? That's what I can't see at the moment."

"So what's our next move?"

"For you and I and DC Ruggles to pay a preliminary visit to the Rumbold-Straight stables. Whether they like it or not, they're deep inside whatever crooked game's going on."

Nick was allowed a lie-in that morning. It was nine o'clock before he entered the stables. The great courtyard was empty. Horses looked out at him from some stable doors; others were now outside, at grass or being exercised. He saw no humans. A peculiar thought crossed his mind that they had all deserted him in disgust. Then, from a stable Ray appeared. He saw Nick and scowled.

"Where is everybody?" said Nick.

"About their business," Ray answered and walked away.

Nick did not like this. He ran and caught him up. "Ray, what's the matter with you? We used to be mates."

Ray shook him off. "Mates? With you? After what you've done?"

"I've done nothing."

"You've *spat* on the memory of a great girl. No sooner is she dead than you're off with another. Can't wait, can you, you messy little rat."

"Ray, it's not like that."

"Of course it's like that. But aren't there just some shocks waiting for you, eh? You're going to be very sorry."

"What do you mean?"

He tried to touch Ray's shoulder to turn him round, to look at him face to face. Ray turned all right – with a wild blow with his right fist which Nick saw in time. He swayed out of its way and stepped back.

Ray rushed in, fists swirling. Nick was smaller, lighter, nimbler. He ducked out of their way while he collected his wits. A glancing blow hit him on the side of the head. Nick leapt forward, to try to seize Ray's flailing arms by the wrists. For someone small who made his living working with horses, Ray was surprisingly clumsy. His once-broken leg took movement away. Nick had grabbed his left wrist, and was both trying to seize and get out of the way of his right when he realized they were being watched.

They both calmed down and turned, panting. A police Ford Mondeo stood in the middle of the courtyard. Chase, Kemp and Ruggles were standing there, looking at them curiously.

Chase ignored what he had seen. "Where's the guv'nor?" he said. "He's expecting us."

"Johnny? In the fields with the vet," Ray muttered. "Mirage Oasis has a strain."

The three walked off. Ray turned to Nick. "That'll give them something to think about," he said.

A stable door opened. Drake appeared from inside, carrying a bucket. He took no notice of the two but walked away, following the three policemen.

"Do you think he heard?" said Nick.

"It's no skin off our noses if he did," Ray replied and walked off the other way. Nick watched him with some relief. The fight was evidently over for now. But he was left with the same question: why was Ray taking this to heart so much?

Chase, Kemp and Ruggles found Johnny and the vet, Will Roxley, in the paddock with Mirage Oasis. Alf was leading the horse gently up and down under the vet's careful gaze.

"Ah, you're here," said Johnny, with bad grace when he saw them.

"I've seen all I need," said Will. "Just rest him for a while. I'm not surprised he ran badly yesterday."

"Alf," said Johnny. "Bring the horse back to the stables. Will, I'll see you when this lot have gone." To the policemen – "We'll go back to the office."

On the way, Johnny showed all his dislike of policemen. "Why are you bothering me again? You know we've got nothing to do with the murders, you know Nick's in the clear. Why can't you leave us alone?"

Chase stayed silent. When they reached the outer office, Johnny quickly said to Beryl Lackland, "I'm going into the office with the Inspector. Make these two a cup of tea while they wait with you."

Kemp looked at Chase, who nodded. There was no point in antagonizing Johnny further.

In the office, Johnny sat at his desk. "Well?" he said.

Beryl made tea as requested. She tried conversation with these two forbidding men. They did not seem ones for small talk.

"Don't let us keep you from your work," said Ruggles.

Kemp was looking out of the window. Something occurred to him.

"Mrs Lackland, has anyone new come to work here since we last visited?"

Beryl thought. "Was Mr Drake with us then?"

"You tell us."

"Mr Drake arrived the very day, now I think of it, that poor Margie was found murdered. He's just another stable-lad."

"A convenient time to arrive," said Ruggles. "Why then?"

Beryl looked confused. "That's not quite true, what I said just then," she said. "It wasn't coincidence. I know why because I'm Johnny's secretary. Alf knows. But nobody else does."

"Know what?" said Kemp.

"No, I mustn't tell you. It's confidential."

"Mrs Lackland," said Kemp. "In a murder investigation, nothing's confidential."

"But Connie and Johnny would give me the sack," said Beryl.

"No, they won't," said Ruggles. "We'll take care of that."

"Sir Norbury Greyling came here without warning that very morning," said Beryl. "He'd heard about the murder and was worried it would bring unwelcome publicity, especially as the one who found the body was riding his horse. He said he smelled the stench of danger." Kemp and Ruggles looked at each other. "He said he was sending a man of his own to watch over his interests here, especially Mornington Sunrise. That horse is very valuable, you know." Kemp nodded. "And the man arrived that day. It was Mr Drake."

"How do you know all this?" Ruggles asked. "Were you in the meeting?"

Beryl looked abashed. "No," she said. "I listened through the door. I knew I shouldn't, but I was so intrigued. But Johnny had to tell me later anyway."

"Why?"

"I didn't have to make up any wages and tax details for Mr Drake. When I asked Johnny why, he told me he was on Sir Norbury's payroll."

She was suddenly interrupted by a loud shout from the office.

"What a load of blithering nonsense!"

"So much for the ringing theory," murmured Ruggles.

14

The door opened. Chase appeared. He stood in the doorway, turned, and spoke to Connie and Johnny.

"I'm sorry, but if you aren't happy about letting us interview people here, we'll take them back to the incident room and that will interrupt your work far more."

There was a wordless grunt from inside and Chase said, "That's settled then. Interviews here."

The three went straight downstairs and sat in the car.

"Unco-operative, both of them," said Chase. "They refuse to countenance the possibility that Sunrise was got at. And I must say I see why. There's been no slip up in security that I can see."

"Did they tell you about Drake?" asked Kemp.

"What about Drake?"

Kemp quickly recounted Beryl's information.

"We can check that," Chase said. "They didn't say. I suppose they don't want to get on the wrong side of their richest client."

"So what now?"

"The vet's still here with Alf Simpkins. We'll talk to them both. We have to speak to Nick Welsh again. And Drake, of course."

"Welsh was having a barney with someone when we arrived," said Ruggles. "That could be interesting."

"A good agenda for the morning," said Chase.

Alf and Will Roxley were just coming back from seeing to China Chimneys. They were not pleased at being interrupted.

Chase was not long with the vet.

"Impossible. Rubbish," was the answer to Chase's direct question. "I know that horse. You're not likely to forget the best animal you're ever likely to meet. Come and see."

He took them to Sunrise's stall. They looked over the door and watched Drake grooming the placidly chewing creature with the gleaming brown, almost black, coat and the pure white blaze running down the forehead between the intelligent, watchful eyes.

"See? Perfect coat, perfect teeth, perfect build. There's no piece of horse-flesh living that comes near him. Absolutely unique. You *can't* substitute him."

Alf was just as adamant. "Couldn't happen. The

horses would have to be switched. But that's impossible inside the stables, and outside I watch him all the time. Drake and me together. And young Ray, of course."

"You know who Mr Drake is?"

"Johnny confided in me. I've kept it from the others, like he said. And Drake watches Sunrise like a hawk."

There was silence. Alf wasn't going to speak any more. Chase tried again.

"Look, let's just imagine there was a switch—"

"There wasn't," said Alf.

"Just for argument's sake. Where could it have happened? On the journey?"

"I drove up with Mornington Sunrise in the single box Sir Norbury Greyling provided himself," said Alf. "Drake was with me in the cab. Ray was in the back. We came straight there – the London Road, then the M3, M25 and M11."

"Not stopping on the way?" asked Kemp.

"It's as much as my job's worth," said Alf virtuously. "Drake wouldn't allow it anyway."

"Not even a quick call in at the motorway services?" said Kemp. "You're only human and it's a long drive."

"I told you. Johnny would sack me," was the reply.

"So what about the night before you left?" asked Chase.

"We've got good security here," said Alf. "Nothing could get in. Nobody could take a horse away without the whole county knowing. Stables have tightened up a lot since Shergar was kidnapped."

"So you're convinced it's impossible," said Chase.

"Of course I am."

Drake next. He was still with Mornington Sunrise. He looked up as they approached.

"Mr Drake," said Chase. "I understand you were with this horse all day yesterday."

"Except when he was running." The voice was harsh, more a growl.

"And you drove with Alf straight there and straight back?"

"Yes."

"You're Sir Norbury's employee, I believe."

Drake did not answer. There was a flash of anger across his face.

"No, don't worry, Mr Drake. Johnny and Alf haven't blown your cover. We'll keep it quiet for you."

Drake fished in his pocket and brought out a plastic card.

"My pass," he said. "Everyone who works for Sir Norbury Greyling has to carry one of these."

"You live over the stables?"

"Yes."

"Has anything suspicious happened during the night?"

"No." Drake's answers were as short as he could make them.

"Are you sure?"

Now he did open up.

"I'm here to watch over Sir Norbury's interests. So I watch everything. If there's something which seems to me in the slightest wrong, I would report back to Scallon Manor like a shot."

"But there's been nothing?"

"Nothing."

"Do you report back regularly?"

"I'll tell you this under duress. I make a coded telephone call every evening to Sir Norbury's personal assistant, Soames. So far, each call has been negative."

"You know we can check on this?"

"Suit yourself."

That seemed to be all with Drake.

"Surly devil," said Ruggles when they were out of earshot.

"Probably why Sir Norbury gave him the job," Chase replied.

Nick was more forthcoming. He was the first not to scoff at Chase's suggestions.

"I woke up this morning thinking it," he said.

"But just a minute," said Ruggles. "You know that horse as well as anybody. You won on him at Buckingham. Surely you'd *know*."

Nick was troubled.

"He was the same. He looked the same and he felt the same to ride. It's just that – well, when I asked him for the extra bit he usually gives so nobody can catch him, it just wasn't there."

"He just had an off-day yesterday," suggested Kemp.

"No. Much more than that. The *one thing* that makes him different from every other horse just wasn't there."

"We've spoken to the vet, we've spoken to Alf," said Chase. "They say it was the same horse."

"Then they must be right," said Nick. "It means I'm finished."

"How do you make that out?"

"They'll say I pulled the race deliberately. I'll lose my jockey's licence and be warned off."

"How can they?" asked Kemp.

"They'll look at race videos. They'll see what they want to see."

"Who's *they*?" asked Chase gravely.

"The Jockey Club at Newmarket. They call the shots in this game."

"But you won yesterday as well," said Ruggles. "You were brilliant on Chucklehead."

"That makes it worse," said Nick. "They know what I *can* do."

"But why should you pull the race?" Kemp was still puzzled.

"They'll look for strange patterns in the betting. If there was a sudden lot of big betting on Artificial Cream just before the off so the odds wouldn't have time to change, they'd find out who was behind it. They'd try to make out these people were paying me to pull the favourite."

"You've got it all worked out," said Chase.

"It's been done before," Nick replied. "I wouldn't be the first."

"Except you didn't," said Chase.

"Of *course* I didn't." Nick's voice suddenly burst out in pure feeling. "This is my life. I love the sport."

They left him soon after, staring disconsolately at the ground, and returned to the car. They sat in it silently for a moment. At last Chase spoke.

"Get on to HQ," he said to Ruggles. "Ask if they'll find out about last minute surges of betting. Not just at Bishop's Stortford racecourse. Try Salebourne betting shops as well. And any others. They could also ask the Jockey Club if they're investigating the betting and Nick's riding."

As Ruggles did so, Kemp saw someone else in the courtyard.

"There's the one Nick was having the ding-dong with," he said. "I'll hop out and have a word."

He left the car and loped across the courtyard. The other two waited. Then Ruggles said, "Look who's coming."

Connie and Johnny were striding purposefully towards them. Chase got out and waited by the car.

"Johnny has a couple of things to tell you," said Connie.

"Yes, Inspector. I'm sorry I blew my top just now. And I'm sorry I didn't tell you about Sir Norbury Greyling's visit here and the arrival of Drake. He told me to keep that secret. Beryl told me she spilled the beans."

"Understandable, seeing who Greyling is," said Chase. "But wrong. Is that all?"

"No, it's not. There are two things which were said to me recently which I can't get out of my mind. There's something Sir Norbury said to me when he was here. 'The stench of danger is here.' Strange phrase. 'The stench of danger'."

"Well, there'd just been a murder. Why were you surprised?" said Chase.

"It's more than that," Johnny insisted. "Coming all that way, putting his own man in here – I went along with it of course, but it seemed an over-reaction. Margie Moxon had nothing to do with him. It's almost paranoid. But he's not. He didn't get to be boss of Kudic and a multi-millionaire by being paranoid."

Chase bit down the retort that paranoia was probably exactly the quality you needed and merely asked, "What are you saying?"

"I'm *sure* there's something more to it."

"Perhaps it's you being paranoid," said Ruggles.

"Perhaps. Wouldn't you be with all that's going on? Especially with the second thing that was said."

"By Greyling?" asked Chase.

"No. Kiteley. It was at Buckingham. O'Keefe had just shaded Nick out on Chucklehead. Nick was furious. I had to calm him down. And then Kiteley came by like a dog with two tails because he'd trained the winner and beaten me into the bargain. And he said, 'You'd better work fast while you still have a licence.' I've thought about that ever since. What did he mean? I'm worried. Especially if there's an inquiry over Mornington Sunrise's running yesterday. If it comes out Nick pulled him, lose my licence is just what I could do."

Chase considered this for a moment.

"You and Kiteley don't like each other, do you?"

"That's got nothing to do with it. No, since you ask, we don't, but I wouldn't do him down. If I get the better of him, it will be fairly. I hope it's the same with him."

"But you're beginning to wonder," said Ruggles.

"Yes, Officer," said Johnny. "What he said was serious. Of course, though, I can't expect you to take it seriously."

"You misjudge us," said Chase. "We'll follow it up."

"I've heard that before." Johnny's voice was jeering. "You'll forget it as soon as you're out of sight."

"Oh, no. It's time we saw Mr Kiteley again."

"Mind you do," said Johnny, and turned on his heel. Before she joined him, Connie gave a gesture with both hands as if to say, "Sorry, you know what he's like."

Chase and Ruggles watched them go to the house. Kemp returned from talking to Ray. "Very interesting," he said.

"Not as interesting as what we've heard," said Ruggles.

"Go on," said Chase.

"Big case of jealousy there. Ray's older than the other stable-lads, except Drake. Wanted to be a jockey, broke his leg in a fall, never been quite right since. He knows he'll never do more than work in a stable if he wants to be with horses. Head lad one day's his limit. I reckon he resents Nick Welsh very deeply."

"Not surprising. Welsh is the blue-eyed boy round here, even after yesterday's fiasco."

"But what really bugs Ling is Nick and Karen Thorpe. The reason's obvious. He carried a big torch for Margie Moxon. Poor Ray. I doubt if Margie ever knew. Or that she'd have taken any notice if she had. But seeing Nick and Karen together the moment Margie was dead, well, that really got up his nose. Right now he hates Nick."

"And in some ways I don't think I blame him," said Ruggles.

"Anything else?" asked Chase.

"Not a lot. That fills his mind. He can't think of other things with that on his mind."

"I see," said Chase. "So is this just a sideshow or part of the maze we've got to sort into a pattern?"

"No idea," said Kemp.

"We have to begin drawing this together," said Chase. "It's all like random happenings building up. No rhyme or reason in them, no connections. We see one lead; the others disappear before our eyes. We're just scratching the surface of a huge design. We've got to burrow deeper before we see a shape. Because there *is* a shape. There's someone behind all this, pulling strings, someone very powerful, ruthless, who'll kill – or make others kill – without thinking twice. But why? What's behind it all?"

There was silence in the car.

"We keep being disappointed," said Kemp. "We thought we might be on to something when you thought about Mornington Sunrise being substituted. Well, that looks like it was wrong. Trainer, head lad, vet, the owner's agent – they can't all be mistaken, surely? And every time we think we're getting somewhere, new bits come, like Nick and Ray—"

"And Rumbold–Straight and Kiteley," said Ruggles as he drove – "which just muddy things up again."

"I know," said Chase. "But among all those things there must be one detail staring us in the face which could tie it all together, *if* we could see it and understand it. Something that's happened. But *what*?"

"Dig deeper still," said Kemp.

"There's one person we've not seen who seems to hover round the outside touching everything that happens just like Nick does," said Chase. "That person we *must* see."

"Who is it?" said Ruggles.

"Sir Norbury Greyling."

Sometimes, Karen really puzzled Nick. He really was crazy about her now, and most of the time she showed she returned the feeling, sometimes overwhelmingly, so he had to catch his breath and remember that even Margie was never quite like that. And then, without warning, she would switch off, be distant, cut him out. She would look away, her eyes would not, it seemed, see him. He would feel truly on his own.

"Karen, what is it?" he cried in some distress.

They were in his room. The Fanshaws didn't like this sort of thing happening, for all the stable-lads were seventeen and more. But wife and husband were away for the night.

Karen didn't answer.

"It's nothing to do with Connie's offer, is it?" he persisted.

"No. That's good of her. I just can't yet."

"Is it about that time when I...? You know, before I started with Margie and you thought it was you I fancied?"

"Forget that," she replied. "It's gone."

She stood up and looked at her watch.

"It's late. Take me home, Nick."

So he did and they walked quietly to her house, with Nick wondering why things were only *nearly* wonderful with her.

As always, it was gone one o'clock by the time he opened the Fanshaws' front gate. No Ray this time on the Honda. Nick was glad, he could do without another row to end the day. He fished in his pocket for the key and then stepped on to the front porch to open the door.

In the darkness, his foot caught something soft but heavy.

A thrill of fear shot through his stomach.

He bent down and touched whatever it was. Cloth. Just a bundle of old clothes Mrs Fanshaw must have left out to be collected for a jumble sale.

He ran his hand further along. No, not just cloth. Something warm, sticky.

He stood up suddenly, heart beating wildly. *Key in the door, dark inside, find the porch light switch, flood the place with light to wash away the fears.* Now he could bend down and see properly the obstruction.

It was the body of Ray Ling, dumped in the porch, his head bloody and broken by a blow from something very heavy.

15

Nick's first instinct was to hide, far away. But he fought it and tried to collect his wits. There was plainly nothing he could do for Ray. So – first thing, call the police. He walked, shaking, to the phone, dialled 999, unsteadily said, "Police, murder," and gave the address. Then he wondered why the rest weren't there. Well, it was Jimmy's night on duty at the stables and Ken often stayed overnight with his girlfriend in Salebourne. A run upstairs and a knock on his door showed that was the case tonight. No, he had to face this all on his own.

He sat on the floor, behind an old dresser where he could not see Ray's body. There would be a few minutes to wait before the police came. He collected his thoughts.

Three murders of people connected with him; he had found them all. This was going to take some explaining. But what had poor Ray done to deserve this?

He caught his breath in horror. *Ray had picked a fight with him that morning and the police had watched.*

Well, that settled it. They'd think he did it. That Inspector would wonder if he'd been too lenient the day he found Margie and Ted, and wouldn't let him go so easily this time.

Yes, but he *hadn't* done it. So who had? Why?

What about the things Ray had been saying? Nick looked in on his own soul. Was Ray right? Was he a filthy rat? Was it so terrible to take up with Karen so quickly? What had Ray found that would wipe the *greasy* – here Nick shuddered at that awful word which couldn't apply to him, surely – smile off his face.

Suddenly, Nick felt revulsion against himself. Going with Karen was selfish, unfeeling, callous. Ray was right: he *was* a filthy rat. He should have cut himself away, mourned for Margie properly. She was worth mourning for. They had been good together.

Ah, but she was two-timing him with that dressed-up half-wit Ted Firs.

What did that matter? Margie was dead, he had loved her and he should have shown proper respect.

And he should have stopped everything to find her killer and exact revenge. Yes, that was what Ray had meant that he shouldn't have had to ask about. But why should Ray want revenge? He thought of Ray alive, small, stocky, with a slight limp, in sight of thirty. And he now saw something so clearly that he'd had no idea of before. Ray must have been blindly, mutely, hopelessly *crazy* about Margie. Now Nick thought of it, every movement Ray ever made shrieked it out. Margie would never know, but it was the great fact of Ray's life.

Nick shuddered. What a terrible way to be.

So Ray *had* gone looking for revenge. And he had found something out – something to *take the greasy smile off Nick's face*.

"Greasy" again. Involuntarily, Nick wiped his lips with the back of his hand as the last awful truth dawned on him.

Ray had been murdered because of whatever it was he had found.

The familiar shrieking of sirens sounded through Matley High Street; there was a squeal of brakes outside. Nick forced himself to stand up, pick his way gingerly past Ray's body and stand by the front gate.

Chase, pulled out of a bed he hardly seemed to have got into, was not in his best humour. Nick could have bet pounds on what he would say.

"Not *you* again!"

Already, detectives were round the body, examining, measuring. Arc lights were set up in the little garden.

"Let's get away from this," said Chase. "We need quiet."

Nick led him into the sitting room. They faced

each other in armchairs either side of the television as if this was to be a pleasant chat.

"Tell me where you found him," said Chase.

So Nick told him of his evening with Karen, when he had left her house, how Karen and her parents would vouch for this.

"But you didn't like the man, did you?" said Chase.

Be careful here. One false move and you'll be in the cells.

"Yes, I did. We were mates."

"It didn't look like that this morning."

"We had a fight. Not much of one. He doesn't – didn't think Karen and I should…" He didn't know quite how to finish the sentence. But Chase seemed to understand what he meant.

"It took you some time to find that out," he said.

"Well, there's more. He said there's other things I should be doing and he was having to do them for me and he'd found out things which would take the smile off my face."

Nick carefully omitted the word "greasy".

"Did he now?" said Chase. "What do you think he meant?"

"He must have found out something about Margie's murder. He never told me what."

"What's that on your hand?" said Chase.

Nick at once lifted his right hand, which he had used to wipe his mouth when he remembered Ray's "greasy".

"No, not that one."

160

He lifted his left.

Incredible. He had reached down to Ray in the dark, had felt his broken head – and had only wiped the blood out of his mind, not off his hand.

"Blood," he said. "Ray's."

"I see," said Chase, suddenly unfriendly. "And is that all the blood of Ray that you've got about you?"

"Of course it is," Nick insisted.

But Chase had called two policemen in and Nick was made to stand up while they minutely examined every inch of his clothing before Chase let them go.

"All right," he said. "The blood tallies with just reaching down and touching him. There's fresh lipstick and make-up on your shirt and jacket which checks out with your story about Karen. No blood spatters as if you'd hit him. Mind you, we'll be going through your wardrobe and the washing machine in case you changed, and through the wheelie bin in case you just threw the incriminating garments away."

Nick sighed with relief.

"After all, you could have gone upstairs, changed, come down again and deliberately touched his head to set this up," Chase continued.

Nick groaned. The four of them tramped upstairs. Nick unlocked his door and put the light on. He gasped.

On the bed, lying in full view on the duvet cover, was a large wrench, such as motor mechanics use.

*　　*　　*

Chase's first thought when he saw the big spanner surprised him. *That's the weapon which killed Ted Firs.* But there were millions of wrenches like this one. Why be so certain? Was this a time for hunches? Just as his instincts were shouting out to him that Nick Welsh was innocent as driven snow of this murder? Or any other? If Nick did it, then leaving the wrench in full view was suicidal. If it was left to frame him, then the attempt was ludicrously unsubtle.

No, there was another reason for its presence there and once again Chase's instincts told him what it might be.

It was a warning to Nick. *Keep out. Don't mess with us.*

And more. *See what happened to Ray.*

Nick sat miserably in the back seat of the police car. He knew another uncomfortable interview awaited him. He looked out, saw Chase talking to a man, obviously the police doctor, considered whether murder could be pinned on him after all. He knew his room was being meticulously turned over, and that so was Ray's.

Chase left the house and came to the car.

"We're taking you to Salebourne," he said. "You can't stay here for the rest of the night. The cells at the police station can be quite comfortable, you'll have a good breakfast and you can go when we've checked out your alibi."

Nick did not answer. Nor did he speak as Ruggles

drove him away. When they arrived, he mumbled answers to the desk sergeant, and then went through what seemed the degrading ritual of handing his belongings over, being led down cold corridors and hearing the cell door clang echoingly behind him. As the key was turned and the constable who had accompanied him trod heavily away he heard snores and shouts to be let out from drunks in other cells.

He lay down and tried to sleep. At least they had given him two blankets and a pillow.

But he couldn't sleep. God, this was the pits. What would it be like if Chase really thought he had done it? Funny about that spanner, though.

Then a horror ran through him. Somebody planted that spanner. If that person wanted to incriminate him, then whoever it was must think he was pretty stupid. But what if the police thought he *was* pretty stupid, had thrown it down in panic, had rung them in a – well, an equally stupid attempt to cover himself? What if that intruder had planted other evidence, more cleverly? What if Inspector Chase came in tomorrow with questions he couldn't answer?

He'd heard of things like this. Sudden evidence after weeks of nothing – so the police nearly kill him with questions and a bit of roughing up, write out a confession he'd be thankful to sign to get a bit of peace – and that was it: murder solved, murderer on trial and being put away for life and his only hope

after the appeal was rejected would be some investig-
ative programme on TV exposing injustices.

No, they couldn't.

But they could. All murderers are supposed to
make one mistake. What if they tried to say his was
thinking he'd be in the clear by being the one to *find*
the body. Once perhaps. Twice – just. *Three times?*
Pull the other one.

Another realization came like a bucket of cold
water in his face. Finding all those bodies could not
be coincidence. It had to be that he was *meant* to find
them.

Why? There was only one possible reason. Whatever was happening here, he was at the centre of it, it
concerned him, someone was after him. What for?
To scare him? To kill him?

But until now he hadn't been scared. Should he
have been? *Yes, he should, right from the start.*

So, why hadn't he even thought of this before?
What had taken his mind off it? He considered the
reason.

Well, the answer was the same as for why he hadn't
spent the last weeks in ceaseless grieving for Margie.
Karen was there: Karen had comforted him, loved
him, brought him back, made him feel good in
himself.

Thank you so much, Karen.

Then a very strange thought came. He didn't
recognize it for a moment. When he did, he tried to
damp it down. But it wouldn't be kept under. It

spread and spread like a cancer.

He was in danger – terrible, terrible danger. Death was on all sides, violent, unreasoning, punctuating his life like commas in the wrong places, marking the time until the cruel full stop. It had been so since he had lifted that white sheet and seen the face of Margie. And he should have realized this from the very start.

But he hadn't. He had gone swanning along without a care in the world. Riding his horses, winning races, losing on Mornington Sunrise and being virtually sacked by Sir Norbury Greyling had taken up all his thoughts. But this getting on with his life as if nothing was happening was stupid. Only an *idiot* wouldn't be scared out of his wits. And he wasn't an idiot.

Or was he? What had made him like this?

Karen.

A few moments ago it had been, "Thank you so much, Karen." Now it was, *Karen, I'm in danger. You're making me forget it. So you're putting me in more danger.*

Yes, but she doesn't mean to do that.

Doesn't she? Who says so?

This was what made him turn face down on the bed in the cell, push his face into the pillow and beat his fists on the lumpy mattress. Was Karen deliberately distracting him so he wouldn't be inquisitive? Oh, how right poor Ray had been! He should have gone looking for revenge for Margie, not letting his days slip by in an ecstasy of snogging and worse. He should have been saying *Why? Why? Why?*

Did Karen know she'd done this?

Of course she did. She was there, spot on, as if waiting for him and knowing exactly where he would be. She knew *precisely* where to go that morning to find Ted Firs. Was she surprised to find him dead? And now Ray was dead – Ray, who had obviously got it in for Karen just as much as for him and who really had found something to wipe the greasy smile off his face. So that was why he was murdered. It *must* be.

And Karen? She worked with Margie; she knew everything about her. She had known all about Ted Firs. She *must* have known more than she told the police.

Oh, God. Karen, his supposed wonderful new girlfriend, was a triple murderer. Why? Jealousy of Margie and Ted, the need to shut Ray up. She must have done them all.

Treachery. Sheer, evil teachery. And he had fallen for it. *Why* was she destroying him like this?

There could be one reason and one reason only. He'd thought about it so often recently – that summer evening before he was set up with Margie, when he had let Karen think that it was she and not Margie who he wanted…

He closed his eyes. He'd brought it all on himself.

And now there was the rest of the night to get through before he could tell the Inspector all this. Because he would have to. Oh, yes, he would have to.

166

Shopping his girlfriend. How low could you get? And yet...

Suddenly, he almost saw Margie beside him. Another summer evening. Just a few weeks ago. He remembered it so clearly. For almost the first time since her murder he was recalling her in detail. They lay side by side on the grassy bank of the river in Salebourne. Boats passed, birds sang. Nick was supremely happy. And Margie had murmured in his ear, "Nick?"

"Yes?"

"It might not always be like this, you know."

"Yes, it will. Always."

She had laid her finger on his lips.

"Things could happen, Nick. Things you wouldn't like."

"Never."

"I hate what could happen. I want to stop it coming to you."

"I'm on the way up. *Nothing's* going to happen to me."

"No. I'll make sure it doesn't. And there's Karen."

Nick had sat up suddenly. "What about Karen?"

"Oh, nothing," Margie had said. "Except that she might just surprise you."

"How?"

"Don't worry. I'll make sure nothing happens to you. Even if it happens to me instead."

A vivid, painful memory. And through all these late events he'd never really thought about it. But it was only now that he was beginning to think about Margie rationally again. Her face disappeared and he felt even more alone in the cold cell.

For a moment. For once again came that recurrent obsession: the two main owners in his life, the two merging faces. Billy Boney and Sir Norbury. He had to work out why he kept seeing them in his mind's eye, why they wouldn't go away. And why had they returned as soon as his memory of Margie's cryptic warning had left him? There was reason for it; subconscious minds don't always work randomly.

The two couldn't be connected? Could they? Never, surely. Could there possibly be in the whole world two people who had less in common? And were they even alike? No, of course they weren't.

Then the two faces merged into one again.

Yes, they are.

There were things beyond him here. He had to get some sleep. He stretched out on the hard bed and closed his eyes. Before he mercifully drifted off, one last thought came.

Now there really is something to tell the police in the morning.

16

Nick was out of his interview with Sergeant Kemp not knowing quite what to think any more. He was given breakfast in the cell, then allowed a shower. Much refreshed, he had been quite disappointed to find Inspector Chase not there.

"He's got to get *some* sleep, you know," Kemp had said.

Even so, he had poured out all he had thought in the night and Kemp had listened.

"I'll tell the Inspector," he had said when Nick recounted the evening by the river with Margie, and then his recurring vision of Billy and Sir Norbury. When Nick had finished Kemp looked at him in disbelief.

"Are you telling me you think your girlfriend has committed these murders? And that the nation's top comic and businessman respectively are involved in a series of messy killings?"

"I don't know. I think I must be. Yes, I am."

"Well, forget it. If Karen's alibi checks out, she couldn't have been near Ray Ling when he was murdered. Unless the two of you did it together. After all, it's you who's given her the alibi."

Nick's relief was profound. A smile lit up his face.

"No, son, don't you worry about your girlfriend. She's solid for you. I've seen you together, remember. I can tell. So what you've said to me is our secret. Nobody else will know."

Well, if the sergeant thinks so... But that wasn't all.

"What about the other thing?"

"I don't know what you're getting at. I can't believe two top people are going around murdering victims they've never heard of. Are they supposed to be in league with your Karen?"

Nick felt stupid. Yes, it was ridiculous.

"You know what it is," said Kemp. "Those two are your opposite poles. One thinks you're marvellous, the other wants you out. They're the most important people to you – even more than Johnny. He's only your boss. No wonder you've got them both on the brain."

Well, put like that...

"But you've got to be careful. You could be in danger. Not from those three. There are others far worse. So keep your eyes in the back of your head."

"I will, Sergeant Kemp, I will."

"And look after that girl of yours," Kemp called after him as Nick walked out into the open air.

Inspector Chase had finally staggered back into bed at four that morning. By ten he was back on duty with one resolve in mind. Yesterday he had said there was someone as much at the centre of things as Nick was. Sir Norbury Greyling. Today he was sure that a long talk with Sir Norbury was about the most important thing on the agenda if he wanted to push this case along any further.

"Later," he had said to Kemp when the sergeant tried to tell him about his talk with Nick.

Where would Greyling be found? At Kudic plc's huge, glass-fronted London headquarters? At home in Scallon Manor, thirty miles away? At home in the chalet in Switzerland? At home in the Manhattan apartment? At home in the yacht off Monaco?

That was the trouble with the very rich. Too many homes.

The Scallon Manor number was ex-directory. But Chase had ways of finding out. Soon he was talking to Sir Norbury's personal assistant.

There was silence at the other end; he was obviously asking his employer. Three minutes later he spoke again, in a suave, educated voice. "Sir Norbury is always anxious to co-operate with the police. We will give you half an hour at two o'clock this afternoon."

Right. Just time to sort out exactly what to ask.

*　　*　　*

It was amazing how much better those few words with Sergeant Kemp had made Nick feel. He wanted to see Karen, to apologize to her for all he had thought, even though she didn't know. How *could* he have entertained such fantasies?

He was sitting on the bus. He looked at his watch. 9.30. She would be at the kids' stables by now. He'd go there as soon as he reached Matley. The bus started. To the background noise of the diesel engine, Nick tried to work things out. How thankful he was that Karen seemed exonerated from treachery. And how silly to imagine Sir Norbury and Billy as a murderous duo. That *must* have been at the back of his mind even though it took Sergeant Kemp to give form to the notion. But he had to be far more alert, aware. He was in danger. And there was a score to settle – for him to settle – with the murderer of Margie. So, no distractions now, he had to go looking, to take on Ray's mantle. Whatever Ray had found, he must find. And he knew the dangers. He could take care of himself.

The day was overcast. September was here and autumn round the corner. Doncaster beckoned. Well, if he was still riding, Johnny would find him some mounts. But no Mornington Sunrise and no St Leger. He would have to wait for his first classic.

Mornington Sunrise. Yesterday he had woken up with the thought that the horse he had lost so badly on was not Sunrise. He'd expressed as much to

172

Inspector Chase. But as the day went on, he'd for-gotten it. What a stupid idea. The horse at Johnny's stables was so obviously Mornington Sunrise. He had just been off colour. Sir Norbury Greyling must soon forget his suspicions that Nick had pulled the race.

The bus reached the terminus in Matley High Street. Nick got off, feeling much better, and started the walk towards the riding school. Not thirty metres from the bus stop was Moxon's Saddlery. With a sinking heart, Nick realized that to reach the riding school he would have to walk past it. Mr Moxon was still the last person he wanted to see. He quickly crossed the road to remain unobserved. Too late.

"Nick." A man's voice came from the shop door-way. Margie's father.

Nick carried on as if he hadn't heard.

"Nick. I know it's you. Come here a minute."

The voice was not unfriendly. I can't keep dodging him for ever, Nick thought. Taking a deep breath, he turned and faced him.

"We've not seen you since ... oh, come in anyway. Have you been avoiding us?"

Still no sign of anger. Mystified, Nick followed him into the dark interior smelling of leather and dubbin. The once big, red-faced man was bowed, old-looking, grey-faced.

"Where have you been all this time? Why didn't you come back to the house after the funeral? We wanted you there."

Margie's mother had joined her husband in the shop. She too looked twice her age. Nick tried to imagine what they must have been through. He stood facing them, lost for words, not expecting what Mrs Moxon did next.

"Nick!" she cried, then threw her arms round him and kissed him on the cheek.

Nick could not understand this. "But aren't you angry with me?" he stammered.

"Why should we be?" asked Mr Moxon. He looked genuinely puzzled.

"Because I started going out with Karen the moment Margie was…" He couldn't bring himself to say "dead" in front of them, let alone "murdered".

"I don't understand," said Mrs Moxon.

"But isn't that why you sacked Karen?" By now Nick was completely baffled.

"I never sacked Karen," said Mr Moxon. "Whatever gave you that idea? She was going off to a new job anyway."

"You mean at the riding school?"

"Which riding school? No, she'd got herself a job at Arthur Kiteley's."

It was nearly an hour before Nick could get out of the shop. The Moxons were really pleased to see him. Their grief over Margie was not less, but it was thawing. They could talk about her, and wanted to. It would help them. And now, suddenly, Nick found his own tongue unloosed. He could talk about her as well and, for the first time since he had found her body, the tears flowed unchecked.

Mrs Moxon was very keen to make one thing clear. "Nick, we had no idea about this other man, this Ted Firs. She never mentioned him to us. We thought she was only for you."

"I *know* she was," Mr Moxon growled.

"And we were so pleased. She had found a good boyfriend who would calm her down."

"I'm no good. I went off with Karen straight away."

"Even if you did, we'd have tried to understand," said Mr Moxon. "I just wish you'd spoken to us at the funeral."

And why didn't he? What wonderful people these were. Here was yet another reason to find Karen.

Business was building up. Their talk was punctuated by customers.

"We'll let you go, Nick," said Mrs Moxon. "Come round and see us one evening."

"I will," Nick promised.

"Soon," she called out as he hurried down the High Street.

But his mind was a whirl. Karen *was* treacherous. Deeply so.

Kemp was filling Inspector Chase in on the events of the night and morning.

"If Ling wasn't killed by that spanner, it was by something very like it," he said. "It comes back to your old idea about Margie and Ted dying in a garage. But nobody seems to have seen anything last night. The Fanshaws were away, one lodger was on duty at the stables, the other was in Salebourne all night with his girlfriend."

"I might have known it. Anything else?"

"I talked to Welsh this morning. He was in a state. He seemed to think his girlfriend had done it."

"Even though he was with her all the time until he came home?"

"We saw her first thing this morning. What Nick said all checks out."

"So where are we?"

"There's another thing. A few months before Margie was murdered, she said to him – let's see, I've got the gist written down here." He looked for the statement form. "Here it is. 'Things you wouldn't like could happen to you. I hate them and want to stop them. I'll make sure nothing happens to you even if it happens to me. Watch Karen. She may surprise you'."

Inspector Chase was suspicious. "You mean she said all that to him and he never told us?"

"He says it all slipped his mind. Don't you believe him?"

"Well, the mind plays strange tricks, I suppose. Perhaps he didn't want to remember it. After all, she as good as said she would die to protect him. Not a nice thought to live with. I shall have to think about it."

"There's something else, though I don't rate it. He's got what I can only call an obsession. He seems convinced there's some deep connection between Greyling and this comedian fellow, Boney. I told him it was just because he rode their horses. He seemed content with that."

"Are you?" said Chase.

"I think so."

Chase thought. "Yes, so am I. Greyling and Boney yoked together? I don't buy it."

It was time for a meeting with the whole team. This took him nicely until an unhealthy meal of sausage, beans and chips in the canteen and then the drive to Scallon Manor.

Once in the open air, Nick could once again think only of Karen. She *must be* playing some sort of dirty game. His night fears were correct. Now he knew she had lied to him. What's more, she was working with the enemy. And something else. No wonder she had gone all cagey when he put Connie's offer to her. She was already working for Kiteley – probably already booked in to the Newmarket course.

He stumbled out of the village towards Kiteley's stables. Baffled anger shook him, stopped him thinking straight. So he was still four hundred metres away – or two furlongs out – from Kiteley's when he started to think rationally.

I'll never be let in. I'm Johnny's man. I'm O'Keefe's rival. They hate me.

He looked up and down the road. No traffic. The bare Downs stretched away on either side, the grey sky lowered. The fences and buildings of Kiteley's establishment stood like an armed fortress.

He was useless, powerless, probably doomed. This was the lowest point of his life so far.

Inspector Chase rang the bell of the vast front door. He had decided before he parked his car that as he held commissioned rank he would use no tradesmen's entrance. A maid appeared and showed him to an ante-room. The owner of the voice on the telephone arrived, looking at his watch. He was tall, dark-suited.

"Admirable punctuality," he said in that same languid drawl.

Watch it, sonny, thought Chase.

"Sir Norbury will see you now."

Chase was led into an immense study. Sir Norbury sat behind a vast, shiny desk. Chase felt intimidated at once.

But Sir Norbury rose and walked towards two armchairs either side of an Adam fireplace. He motioned Chase to sit and sat opposite. Chase was at once at ease.

"Now, Inspector," Sir Norbury said.

Chase came straight to the point. "Sir Norbury, when you visited Mr Rumbold-Straight, you said you recognized the 'stench of danger'. May I ask what you meant by that?"

"A young girl murdered and a young man with her, should be danger enough I would have thought."

"Forgive me, Sir Norbury, but I think you meant more than that."

"There is danger everywhere."

"You mean you have enemies?"

"It would not be surprising, would it?"

Chase knew a dead end when he saw it. He tried another tack.

"Does the danger include your horse Mornington Sunrise and its young jockey?"

Anger showed in Sir Norbury's face. "That's not danger. That's cheating. I'll have that young man ruined. I shall be contacting the Jockey Club this afternoon. They'll set up an inquiry. It can have only one outcome. Welsh is finished."

"I was at Bishop's Stortford," said Chase. "I saw the race. And I'm not so sure."

"I see. You are an expert on racing?"

"Far from it. But I think I know human nature. And I don't believe there's a dishonest thought in Nick Welsh's head. Foolish, maybe."

"Unless he is injured, a great horse always comes through. Sunrise was held back."

I'll try my idea on him, thought Chase. *Nobody believes it, but I won't let go.*

"Have you considered that the horse running that day was *not* Mornington Sunrise?"

Sir Norbury looked baffled. "What do you mean?"

"Another horse was substituted for him."

"You mean you think we're dealing with a ringer? The ancient art of the horse-faker?" Sir Norbury laughed, without humour. "Impossible."

"Why?"

"Because I chose Rumbold-Straight's stables for their security as much as their excellence. And because my own man is there to guard against such happenings – my own trusted employee in the stables to keep watch over all my interests."

"You mean Drake?"

"I do. He reports every evening to Soames, my personal assistant. So far, all is well. I must ask you to treat this as confidential."

"So ringing is impossible."

"Absolutely."

"And yet the stench of danger has not gone. Four murders now – and though there's no circumstantial link I'm positive they're connected somehow with Mornington Sunrise."

"So what do you want me to do?"

"Nothing. Leave it to us."

Sir Norbury was silent for a moment, considering. Then: "Very well. I won't dismiss what you say. I will delay contacting the Jockey Club for forty-eight hours. Welsh has a stay of execution."

Chase knew that was as much as he could expect. But this interview was far from over. He cudgelled his brains for the next move.

17

Nick had no idea how long he just stood blankly by the side of the empty road. He was beyond wondering how to get into Kiteley's stables. Tainted by murder, swindled by his girlfriend, career in ruins – what was the point? He was just a fool, the world's laughing stock. The next vehicle that came by, he'd just stand in front of it and that would be that.

But no vehicles did go by. Once past Kiteley's stables, the road petered out in a tiny hamlet in the Downs. And when a vehicle finally did come, he recognized it. The nine-horse transporter from Matley Racehorse Transport. And from over a hundred metres away he knew who would be driving it. Len Roach.

So he did step out into the road. But not to be run over. He waved his arms for Len to stop. When the big truck hissed to a halt, Nick had a sudden instinct that his low point had been passed.

Len opened the cab door and looked down. "What's up, mate?"

"You must be going to Kiteley's," said Nick.

"Of course. Loading up horses to take to the sales. Some owner's gone bankrupt. Kiteley won't like that."

"Give us a lift there, will you?"

"You? Go to Kiteley's? He'd set the dogs on you."

"That's why I need a lift. I've got business there. Kiteley mustn't know. I'll crouch down so no one will see me."

"All right, but if you're found it's nothing to do with me, see? You stowed away and I never knew. Keep me out of it."

"A deal," said Nick, and climbed up the passenger side. He crouched out of sight as the transporter lumbered off again, to be stopped after hardly a minute. He heard gates open, voices, Len saying, "Dead on time. We don't let you down," and then the transporter bumped over rougher ground until it came to a halt.

"Slip out now," whispered Len. "And don't let anyone see you or I'll get the sack."

Nick opened the door his side. There were voices, the sounds of whinnying and hoofs clopping. They were all from the other side of the transporter. He could see no humans, no horses. A line of stables stood before him, a gate next to them. Carefully, he climbed down to the ground and crouched behind the transporter's front wheels. Dare he make a dash to the cover of a stack of six bales of hay by the end stable door next to the gate?

He waited for the moment. The voices urging the horses in continued. He heard the change in noise as the horses climbed up the wooden ramp. They would soon be loaded up. If he didn't move soon he might be flattened by a motor vehicle after all.

Then he recognized two human voices in particular above the clatter and whinnying of horses. One was Kiteley's: the sharp, unfriendly bark. The other was Karen's.

It was now or never. They wouldn't see or hear him above this noise. He dashed the twenty metres to the hay bales, feeling very exposed. The stack was high enough for him to stand behind unseen. He saw Kiteley standing there, giving orders. He saw stable-hands leading horses who did not want to go, cajoling, soothing, calming them. One of the stable-hands was Karen.

The sight made his stomach turn. All the while he had talked to the Moxons, he had told himself they just might have got it wrong. Not much hope – they weren't daft – but just a little something to cling to.

But actually to see her as if she was at home in the place, used to Kiteley – even on good terms with him, if such a thing were possible – pushed him right back in the depths again. He had been taken for a ride, made a fool of, by the one he trusted most. *Why?*

He realized now that he didn't quite know what he was doing here. What had his plan been? Like a knight of old, to rescue Karen from Kiteley's evil clutches? Fat chance. No, he was back in the pits, worse than ever. He wanted to lean on the hay bales and cry his heart out. Except that the noise would give him away.

So he stood quiet, considering. He needed to talk to Karen. Why not wait until this evening? No. *Now*, to catch her off-guard. She'd get the shock of her life and he'd have the upper hand. But how? He had to put his misery and anger behind him and think rationally. For a moment he managed to lose himself in working out strategies, each of which he dismissed as useless.

Suddenly there was a wet, warm, rasping, not unpleasant, oddly familiar sensation at the back of his neck. Anyone not used to horses would have jumped a metre in the air at it. Nick merely put his hand up to the head of the horse leaning over the door behind him and said "Stop it" absent-mindedly.

Then: *what horse here, in these alien stables, would show me friendship?*

He turned. Brown eyes in a long, wise head looked at him, then reached forward again with a tiny whinny of pleasure to nuzzle him.

He stared. He had never seen this horse before. Its head was a uniform, unbroken dark brown. But there was something about those perfect teeth, those clear intelligent eyes that reminded him so much of

Mornington Sunrise.

But this horse was not Mornington Sunrise. Sunrise had that distinctive white blaze down his forehead. Yet this horse knew Nick. More. This horse trusted Nick. That was almost a nuzzle of recognition, uncannily like the nuzzle of consolation when he found Margie's body and the nuzzle of victory after the Gawcott Stakes. But Mornington Sunrise was in his stable at home, probably being groomed by Drake. He was, he was.

So why did a horse he'd never seen before nuzzle him so affectionately?

He looked hard at the unfamiliar head, then deep into the – yes, they *were* familiar eyes. And those eyes seemed to pass a message out to him – "I am Mornington Sunrise. Please take me away from here and bring me home."

But the head was not the head of Mornington Sunrise. Nick stood irresolute for a moment. Karen, Kiteley, all the other stable-hands, Len – they were gone. Perhaps to a cup of coffee in the office while Len signed the papers giving him responsibility for his cargo? Nick did not want to speak to Karen now. He had a new situation to deal with. He made his mind up. If this horse was, mystifyingly, Mornington Sunrise, there was no talking to Kiteley or Karen about it. He had to get the news out – to Johnny and to the police.

He must get back in the transporter while there was time. He stroked the horse's head again, said,

"All right, old chap. I'll see what I can do. Goodbye for now," and three seconds later was crouching on the floor of the cab waiting for Len to return.

"You were quick," Len said as he headed back towards Matley.

"I've done all I wanted," said Nick. "And I didn't want to get you in trouble. So you owe me a favour. Could you drop me at Johnny's?"

"I owe you nothing," said Len. "You owe me. It's out of my way but, yes, I will."

So ten minutes later, Nick stood in another court-yard outside another stable block. Yes, Sunrise was in there. Alf and Drake were with him.

Alf saw Nick first. "Police let you go, have they?"

"They had no cause to keep me," said Nick.

But there were other things on Alf's mind. "Poor old Ray," he said. "I can't believe it."

Alf was very upset. What Nick wanted to say seemed trivial. But he had to.

"Alf, I've been to Kiteley's."

"I don't believe you."

"You have to. Never mind why. And there's a horse there uncannily like Sunrise. No white blaze on his forehead—"

"Then how can he be Sunrise? Don't talk stupid," Alf interrupted.

"But he *knows* me, he nuzzles me just like Sunrise did."

Nick leaned over and stroked the head of the horse in the stable, resplendent with white blaze. And he realized something that eluded him at Bishop's Stortford. "This horse doesn't know me," he said.

"Finding all those bodies has sent you doolally," Alf muttered.

Nick remembered something Alf had told him. "It's almost as if this horse were his identical twin."

Alf straightened up. He looked quite angry.

"I told you. The twin is dead. Put down. I *know*. It's all recorded. Vet's signature and all. He was pedigree, bloodstock. It's on lists at Newmarket."

Nick felt deflated. "Yes, I know," he said.

All this time, Drake had done no more than gently run a brush around the horse's back. But now he spoke. Nick realized it was the first time he had ever heard this deep, almost menacing voice.

"I would be very surprised if this were not the horse I have been attending since I came here."

Nick felt foolish. Of course they were both right. Horse's brains weren't that big. He'd been under orders to keep away from Sunrise, so perhaps the horse had just forgotten him. And that business at Kiteley's? Accidental. That horse just took a fancy to him.

No, it was Karen he should have worried about. And he'd just lost the chance to catch her really off-guard.

"Anyway," Alf said. "You're not supposed to be here. Get off home and put some sense back into your head."

Nick trailed off. He was past understanding what

was happening to him. Alf was sure – and Drake must know. Mustn't he? But there *was* a hint of menace in that voice – was it a coded signal for "Let it be, don't pry any further"?

No, he would not let it go. Before he was out of the courtyard, he looked back and shouted, "I *am* right. I'm going to the police."

The interview had almost dried up in embarrassed silence. Chase expected Sir Norbury to say, "I think this should be terminated." Instead, he seemed to be waiting, as if presuming another move would be made and disappointed because it was not.

Chase decided to come clean. "Sir Norbury," he said. "I'm here because I believe the murders so far – and there has been a fourth, of a young stable-lad who often attended Mornington Sunrise – are actually motivated by events surrounding your horse."

"And I think, Inspector, that is fanciful speculation."

"No more fanciful, dare I say, than your 'stench of danger'. In fact, I believe my suspicions *are* your stench of danger. And I believe you think so too."

"You say four murders," said Sir Norbury. "Including this latest, I am only aware of three."

"A fourth man was found in the river near Salebourne. His features had been made unrecognizable."

"I see. And what connects it with the others?"

"Nothing as yet. But I am sure in my own mind that it is."

"Your forensic processes seem puny in the extreme," said Sir Norbury.

"Perhaps. That's why I'm here."

They were sparring. Chase had to find an opening. If none appeared, he would have to take a chance and bludgeon his way through. Sir Norbury was not going to help him. He made his mind up.

"Sir Norbury, I wonder if we might consider for a moment whether the link is yourself?"

Sir Norbury's eyebrows lifted. "May I ask how that might be?"

Ah, but you know, thought Chase. *I'm right and it scares you.*

"You are rich and important. You must have many enemies."

"In business, many. I know who they are and can deal with them."

He'll give nothing away, thought Chase.

"And, of course, you are far too well-established to be threatened with ruin through business," he said.

"Why do you say *ruin*?"

"If you smell danger, it follows that you are *in* danger. Of what? Probably not murder. It would have been done by now without need to mow down others beforehand. No, the danger is of ruin: personal, social, in the end, human ruin."

"I have told you. I know my business enemies."

"I am not talking about business."

"Then what?"

"The public know you better than they know most

189

tycoons. They know you through your racing, your horses, your love of the sport. If you're to be ruined in the eyes of the public, then through horse-racing it will be."

Sir Norbury was silent. He looked away from Chase for the first time. *Got it in one*, Chase exulted.

"Sir Norbury, is there anyone who might want to destroy you in this way?"

"Of course not." The answer was hoarse. Suddenly, Chase was in full charge of the interview.

"Are you quite sure? Think, please."

The answer came after fifteen seconds of almost unbearable silence.

"Inspector, there is only one person of whom I have ever been afraid."

Silence again. "Who might that be?" Chase said at last, almost gently.

"It was many years ago. My elder brother."

Silence again. This was going to be hard.

"Yes?" said Chase.

"Inspector, don't think I haven't made enemies. I have made many. But none that I fear – or even hate. I would be surprised if enemies in business really hate or fear me. When all is said and done, what is it but a big game?"

"Many people's livelihoods depend on it," murmured Chase.

"You mean this is a conspiracy of the newly redundant?" Sir Norbury said. "I doubt it. No, the real feelings, the fears and hates which matter, start in childhood."

Chase said nothing. Let this man talk in his own time.

"Unlike many of the super-rich, I did not start with five shillings and a barrow in the East End. I was born to a family, firm, solid, prosperous, not rich but comfortable. Kenton, my elder brother by three years, should have inherited the firm; I should have had a good sum of money and the promise of a job for life in it. I would have been content with that. But I couldn't help it that I was my mother's favourite and – probably because of that – my father's also. I couldn't help it that as the years went on this discrimination between the two of us became more and more obvious, or that Kenton became more and more hurt and aggressive. Nor do I blame him for this. How my parents acted was damaging to both of us. Being favoured gives no help to the favourite. Even then it seemed unfair. Throughout my childhood I actually tried to annoy my parents, to make them *like* Kenton. My attempts always failed; unerringly, Kenton was blamed. 'Give a dog a bad name' never had a truer illustration. I won't bore you with details. I can't blame Kenton for hating me. Apart from an early love of horses, we had nothing in common. He was wild, I was ordered and calm. But I never tried to do him hurt. However, he thought I did. To speak your language, Inspector, he thought at first that I was 'framing' him for any misdemeanours for which he was held responsible. The irony was, I *wanted* to get into trouble, to take the pressure off him – my way of living a calm life. Inevitably, things worsened. The family was blighted. Kenton spent his teenage years in open rebellion; so much so that our father publically disinherited him. That was always a threat; we never believed it and Kenton was foolish enough to test it out. I was as shocked as he was to find our father meant it. When he died just after my twenty-first birthday I inherited the firm and found myself a considerable businessman already. Kenton was cut out as if he never existed. That day was the last time I saw him – or even heard of him. But I remember his final words to me. 'One day you will lose everything, including your very will to live'."

Had he finished? Chase waited.

"Those were words to give anyone pause, don't you think, Inspector? They certainly stopped me in my tracks. Everything I've ever done since has been fuelled by them. The need to turn Greyling Brothers into Kudic plc, the compulsion to turn my love of horses and racing into nationwide fame, the need to be *known*. The need, if you like, to make it impossible that I will ever lose my will to live."

The silence made Chase think he could speak again.

"Where is your brother now?"

"I've no idea. He disappeared. I've tried to find him, to offer him a truce, peace, a share in all I have. But Kenton Greyling seems to have disappeared from the earth."

"Perhaps he has. Perhaps he is dead."

"Inspector, I *know* he is not dead. I *know* he will choose his time and make his threat real."

"Do you think that is what is happening now?"

"I am sure of it."

Chase looked at the large, grey-haired, square-faced man and thought, *I must take this seriously. I believe my hunches so I should believe his.*

"So you are saying to me, 'Find my brother and you find the source of the stench of danger'?"

"Yes, Inspector, I am."

"Yet you have no advice to give me about where to start looking?"

"None whatever. For the first time in my life, I am completely powerless. He will have taken on any guise, use any name. He'll be a person of some consequence, you can be sure of that. We are not fools in the Greyling family."

"Might your mother know?"

"She died ten years ago. She never acknowledged his existence after he left."

"So you agree with me that the murders, the trouble surrounding Mornington Sunrise, everything else, is directed at you."

"I do."

"So why go out of your way to destroy poor Nick Welsh?"

"Because the only way to find who is paying him is to haul him up in front of the Jockey Club. That will *scare* it out of him."

"Even if there is nothing to find?"

"What is happening now will only be the start. My brother is behind it and his route towards my destruction will be long and tortuous and I will look on, powerless to stop it."

"I see." Chase wanted to go now. He had a lot to think about. The most important matter was what, if anything, he should now do about all that he had just been told. Some would say it was pure paranoia. He would not go so far. Not yet, anyway.

He stood. "Sir Norbury, thank you for your time. You have given me much food for thought. Of course, I shall treat all that you have said as confidential. I will be in touch."

He rose and left the room. Outside was Soames, the personal assistant. Chase remembered something that he needed to check on.

"Mr Soames, how does Drake at the Rumbold-Straight stables keep in contact?"

"He rings me every evening. A coded telephone call. I report at once to Sir Norbury."

"And so far there's been nothing out of the ordinary?"

"Nothing."

Chase walked thoughtfully to his car. As he pulled his belt on and started the engine, a question crossed his mind. Was there a connection between Greyling's visit to Johnny, Drake's entry to the stables on the same day and the unknown body in the reeds?

18

It seemed a long way from the stables to the incident room set up at the old chapel in the High Street. Nick used it as a training run; weight down, strength and stamina up, that was the motive to keep in his head all the time. Even these events mustn't let him forget. The day was still overcast: a few drops of rain fell. His wins had brought him a bit of bonus money above the usual apprentice wages; it was about time he thought of a car and driving lessons. Or even a little Honda like Ray's.

He caught himself thinking the name and suddenly even his heat from running went. He was cold. More, he was scared. There was a trail of death leading to him, he must be next. Without stopping, he looked back. The empty road stretched through the bare Downs. No sign of life. But now he felt followed, stalked. He could go to the police all he liked. What good would it do?

None. But just pretend it might.

He arrived, burst inside, asked for Chase or Kemp.

"The Inspector's still on the road," said the WPC he spoke to. "I can get him to hurry up."

Chase drove back deep in thought. What had all that added up to? Finding the body in the reeds the day after Drake had arrived might be coincidence, might be significant. But he believed all Sir Norbury had said about Drake – and it was backed up by Soames. What about all that fascinating stuff about a lost brother, though? Was it relevant? Was it true? Could it possibly give credence to Nick Welsh's fixation about Sir Norbury and Boney? He waited for the familiar stab of recognition which would let him know another hunch was on the way which could be trusted.

None came. *You're imagining things, young Nick*, he thought. *I said I didn't buy it and I was right.*

What if Mornington Sunrise had been sub-stituted? Ringing was surely a fraud connected with huge betting fixes. Money would be the aim, surely, not the settling of old scores. But to justify so many deaths, the amounts of money involved must be *huge*. So far, despite putting the team on to finding out, no strange betting patterns had come out about the Puckeridge Cup. Would they with the St Leger?

No, it didn't add up, any of it.

His car-phone rang. He listened, then, instead of going back to Salebourne, took the next turn to Matley.

"I know the horse doesn't *look* like Sunrise," Nick insisted. "But I'm sure it is. He knew me. He nuzzled me on the neck like Sunrise always does, the moment he saw me. No strange horse would do that. And the Sunrise in our stables won't."

"But that horse looks like your Sunrise," said Chase.

He hardly dared believe Nick. Because if he could, the first real breakthrough was here.

"That means Arthur Kiteley's behind it all, doesn't it?" Nick was busy finding consequences. "Johnny won't be surprised."

Chase didn't answer. And in the silence, Nick realized that if Kiteley was, then surely Karen must be as well.

Johnny was furious when three police cars roared unannounced into his stables. Chase calmed him down. Within two minutes, he, Connie, Chase, Kemp and Ruggles, Nick and Alf were outside Mornington Sunrise's stall. Curious stable-lads watched as Alf led the horse out, tall and gleaming, his white blaze bright against the dark brown.

"Of course it's Sunrise," said Johnny. "There's no horse like him in the world."

"But there *was*," said Nick. "Alf, tell the Inspector what you told me about his twin."

"We all know he had a twin," said Johnny. "What's that got to do with it?"

"The twin's dead," said Alf. "I told you that as well."

"Tell *me* anyway," said Chase.

"Mornington Sunrise had an identical twin. Same coat, same blaze, you couldn't tell them apart. But when they were yearlings, it was obvious Sunrise was outstanding, Noonday ordinary. They came up for sale together at the Bloodstock Sales. Greyling bought Sunrise and brought him here."

"Who bought Noonday?" asked Chase.

"I don't know. An agent on behalf of some foreign buyer, probably."

"Then what?"

"Well, I know Noonday came to Kiteley's, I know he broke a leg and was put down."

"*How* do you know, Alf?" asked Chase.

"We head lads stick together," said Alf. "Our guv'nors may be at daggers drawn but that doesn't stop Connors and me having a drink together now and then. He told me one night in the Feathers."

"And you believed him?"

"Of course I believed him. The twin's dead."

"I'll talk to you later, Alf," said Johnny, red-faced with anger. "I expect loyalty."

Connie laid a hand on his shoulder. "Calm down, Johnny. Can't you see Alf was being deliberately led on? And what does it matter, if we've caught Kiteley out once and for all?"

"That settles it," said Chase. "Off to Kiteley's we go – everyone who could identify Mornington

Sunrise. And I want someone to bring a container of turpentine and a soft cloth."

Nick looked round. "Where's Drake?" he said.

"He went just after you were here before," said Alf.

The gate into Kiteley's stables was open. The place seemed very quiet. Nick looked round to see if Karen was there. They found only a couple of stable-lads, looking frightened and confused. No Kiteley, no Karen.

"Where's Mr Kiteley?" Chase demanded.

"In the house," said one.

"Get him out," Chase said to Ruggles. He turned to Nick. "Show me the stable where you say you found Sunrise."

Nick led the Inspector to it. Before he reached it, though, he had a premonition of what he was going to find. Nothing. The stable was bare.

"Search the other stables," Chase ordered.

But before anything could be done there was a shout from the other side of the courtyard, from outside Kiteley's small modern bungalow.

"Sir. The place is empty. So is the garage."

Chase turned and ran towards the bungalow. Inside it was tidy, spotless, run with military bachelor efficiency. Yet also there was the atmosphere of a place no longer lived in.

The two stable-lads stammered out all they knew.

"That man Brown came," said one.

"He was in a tearing hurry," said another.

"Who's Brown?" asked Chase.

"I don't know. He's often here with the guv'nor."

"Surly devil. Never speaks to us."

"He's probably an agent for an owner. Kiteley never told us."

Chase, Johnny and Alf looked at each other. The same thought was occurring to each.

"He came to where we were all working and said he'd got orders from the owner that the horse in the stable at the end had got to be moved. We were to shift it into the new single horsebox that Brown had brought two months ago."

"Which horse was that?" asked Chase.

"Dark brown three-year-old stallion. Nemo, he was called."

"Never heard of him," said Alf.

"He's never raced that I know of," said one of the lads.

"Except Saturday at Bishop's Stortford."

"He never ran at Stortford."

"Then why did Connors take him out?" The two lads were arguing among themselves now.

"Brown's orders. Connors always did what Brown said. You'd think these were Brown's stables sometimes."

"What happened after you put this Nemo in the horsebox?" asked Chase patiently.

"We got back to our work. Connors and Brown went into Kiteley's house. The horsebox just stood there by the stable until Brown and Connors came out together."

"Without Mr Kiteley?"

"That's right. Brown said the guv'nor wasn't feeling too well but the doctor was coming and we weren't to disturb him."

"This Brown," said Chase. "How long has he been coming here?"

The two lads looked at each other.

"Regularly twice a week for months. He and the guv'nor would walk around talking for hours."

"Come to think of it, though, I've not seen him since that day Margie Moxon and Ted Firs were found dead."

Chase had another question. "How did Brown come here?"

"In a black Volkswagen Golf."

"And what car does Kiteley drive?"

"A white Rover." The stable-lad gave the registration number as well.

"Thank you," said Chase. "I'd like to say now that Drake, Brown, whichever he is and probably neither, hears what Nick has to say when he turns up at the stables this afternoon, realizes whatever gaff it is has been blown and gets across here to do as much damage limitation as he can. And that includes getting Kiteley and Connors out of the way. There must be some amazing secrets at stake for all this."

"And Karen's with them," Nick groaned.

"So what do we do?" said Connie.

"DC Ruggles," said Chase. "Put out a call for a single horsebox, black Golf and a white Rover, possibly travelling in convoy, to be picked up."

Ruggles did so and there seemed nothing for Chase and the rest to do for the moment – except wait for news and hope that the horse called Nemo had come to no harm.

And then something happened that nobody, least of all Nick, could have forecast. The gate by the end stable was opened from the other side. Someone was coming in from the paddock.

This someone was leading a horse. For a moment nobody took any notice. Until Nick looked straight at the horse and its guide.

"*Karen!*" he shouted.

"I know," she answered, smugly. "And look who I've got."

The horse was tall, well-muscled, gleaming – a uniform, unbroken, almost black dark brown.

"What are you doing with Nemo, Karen?" said one of the stable-lads. "I thought Connors and Brown took him away."

"Oh, no they didn't," she replied.

"That's the horse I saw this morning," said Nick.

"Well, it's not Mornington Sunrise," said Alf. "There's no white on him."

"Put him back in his stall, Nick," said Chase. Within a minute, the long head was looking at them over the stable door. Pure, dark brown.

"Undo the turps container," said Chase. Ruggles

did so, soaked a cloth in it and handed it to Alf.

"What do you want me to do with this?" said Alf.

"Sponge him very gently on his forehead where Sunrise's white blaze is," said Chase.

"I'll do no such thing. I'm not risking getting that stuff in his eyes."

"Nick?" said Chase.

Nick jumped out of his amazed trance in which he could not sort out whether the reappearance of Karen or the horse was the bigger shock. He so desperately wanted to talk to Karen, to find out what was going on. But it would have to wait. She was here, she was neither escaping with nor a hostage of the man who called himself Drake or Brown and who was probably a multiple murderer.

He squeezed the soaked cloth on the ground, then stood on a bale of hay so he could reach easily. The horse did not shy away as he leaned towards him with this strange-smelling object in his hands but continued to look at him with friendship and trust. Gently Nick dabbed and sponged at the top of the forehead.

The ring of people round him watched in silence which almost crackled.

On the horse's head, nothing changed.

"Keep going," said Chase.

Alf was right. It would be a disaster if this stuff got in the horse's eyes.

And then there was a change at the top of the horse's forehead. The brown was no longer quite so dark. Stain was coming off on the cloth. Nick got down and soaked it again. Yes, lighter and lighter – until there was no doubt. He suppressed a shout of joy when he realized he had uncovered a patch no bigger than a fifty-pence piece of pure white.

"That's enough for now," said Chase. "The rest can come off another time."

Johnny said, quietly and awed, "Mornington Sunrise."

"Then the horse back at Johnny's *is* his twin," said Nick.

"He *can't* be," groaned Alf.

"There's only one explanation," said Chase. "He wasn't put down. Probably didn't even have a fall. It was a put-up job by Kiteley and Connors. Mornington Noonday had his white blaze blacked out and became Nemo, the mystery horse who never raced."

"That can't be right," insisted Alf. "The vet signed the form. We all know Will Roxley."

"I'm afraid that your Will Roxley must have been in it too. He would have been well paid, no doubt."

"But the owner – would he know?" Johnny asked.

"We need to find out who the owner was," said Chase. "This all looks like a conspiracy which has been long in the making." He was beginning to think Sir Norbury Greyling's afternoon outpourings were not paranoia after all.

"But there must have been a switch made," insisted Johnny. "And that's impossible. Mornington

Sunrise was never out of our sight."

Alf was looking at the ground, embarrassed.

"Guv'nor," he said. "I've got a confession to make."

"Go on," said Johnny.

"I told you I never stopped on the way to Bishop's Stortford. And I wouldn't have. Not with Drake breathing down my neck. But as we were coming up the M25, he said, 'Alf, you look a bit tired to me. I'll take over if you like.' 'I'm all right,' I said. 'Well, I reckon you could do with a break. We'll pull up at the South Mimms Services. You and Ray go in and get a coffee. I'll stay here. I'll go myself when you get back. We'll take fifteen minutes each. It's best to get there in one piece.' I remember every word he said. I'd never known him so pleasant. Well, I went off with Ray and thought nothing of it. Why should I? The owner's trusted man was in charge."

"I should have your guts for garters, Alf," said Johnny.

"That's when the switch was made," said Chase. "Did you notice anything different in the vehicle when you got back?"

"Well, it was cleaner inside. Drake said he'd been round it with the car-vacuum we carry. And now you mention it, I'd noticed some clutch slip when we started out. I was going to report it. But it seemed to have sorted itself out after the break so I never bothered."

"So. They had an identical vehicle, simply waited until Alf arrived, drove your horsebox with Sunrise on board away, put the other one with the twin in the same parking space and Alf drove off again none the wiser. Simple, elegant and pretty well foolproof."

There was silence. Then Johnny said, "So who was our Mr Drake?"

"More to the point," said Chase, "whose body was it in the river caught up in the reeds?"

Nick could not wait any longer. He grabbed Karen by the shoulders. "I've been worried *sick* about you. Lying to me, lying to Margie's parents, going with the enemy. What have you been doing? And can I trust you now?"

Karen leaned into his body. He felt her warmth. She had come back to him. "Yes, you can trust me now, Nick. You always could. And I'm sorry about Margie's parents. But I would have let Margie down if I'd done anything else."

This was beyond Nick's understanding. "What do you mean?" he said.

"Later," she said. Chase had questions to ask her.

"Karen, are we to assume the horsebox has been driven away empty?"

"Oh, no," she said. "I knew something was up when this man I'd never seen came storming in and made us load that horse up. I didn't know what was happening, but somehow I was sure I had to stop it. The horse in that stable had always been a mystery to me and I'd noticed I never seemed to get a chance to go near him. Perhaps there was this idea at the back of my mind about who he really was. I don't know. But I did know 'Nemo' was Latin for 'nobody' and that was a bit weird in itself. So I led Nemo – Mornington Sunrise – off again and tied him up round the back of the stable. But I couldn't leave the horsebox empty. Arthur Kiteley has an old hack he uses to trot around the practice run to see what's going on. This horse is big and quite similar in colour to Nemo. So I took him out of his stable and put him in the horsebox instead. I was scared stiff they'd be out before I'd finished. Then I led Sunrise round the side of the stables. I was going to wait a while, then lead him off round the Downs all the way back to Johnny's."

"That could have been classed as horse rustling, young lady," said Chase.

"Oh, no. By then I'd got a pretty good idea I was right."

"And you hadn't seen Brown before?"

"Never. I'd heard of him. And the lads grovelled like he was God himself when he turned up."

"What about Drake?"

"I'd heard a lot from Nick. He was always on about him. But I'd never seen him."

"There's a lot else I have to ask you," Chase began.

"And me," said Nick.

But they never got a chance. A detective-constable ran from a car by Kiteley's bungalow.

"Sir. A horsebox has been found abandoned in a

layby on the A3. There's no driver but there's a horse inside."

"Right," said Chase. "Tell all units to keep looking for the Rover and the Golf. They're likely to have all three of our men inside now. And they must keep an unobtrusive watch on the horsebox."

"What will they be waiting for?" asked the constable.

"I believe someone will pick the horsebox up and take it on. We need to know where they're going to. And tell them I'll be there myself as soon as I can."

19

The police were gone. They had roared off in the early evening sunshine to where the horsebox with the wrong horse inside was waiting for whoever would come for it. Johnny and the others from the stables had cadged a lift home to bring Mornington Sunrise's horsebox back for his triumphant return. The two remaining stable-lads were still there, puzzled and shocked, to see to Kiteley's horses. The entrance to the stables had been sealed off and two policemen stood on guard.

Nick and Karen were now close together in the back of a police car. Johnny had told Nick he need not go back with them, so the pair were dropped in the High Street. Only for a split second did Nick waver between being with Mornington Sunrise or with Karen. More and more questions had come to mind which he must ask Karen, but every time he tried to whisper one in the car, she answered "Later".

Well, now they stood in Matley's High Street. So "later" was here. But where would "later" be?

"Let's sit somewhere and talk," said Karen.

"No. Let's walk."

So they headed out of the village, along a narrow road which led steeply up into the Downs to the north. Soon, Matley's huddled roofs were below them. Darkness was coming; lights were going on. Far to the left were the lit buildings of Johnny's stables. Kiteley's, to the right, were darker now.

They stopped and looked over this panoramic view. Nick realized Karen was trembling. "I thought you were against me. I thought you'd betrayed me," he said.

Karen didn't answer.

"Why didn't you tell me you were working at Kiteley's? Why did you say the Moxons hated me? They never gave you the sack. Why did you say they had?"

"That's enough questions," said Karen.

"You have to tell me the answers," Nick replied.

Impulsively, she threw her arms round him and buried her head in his shoulders. She was still trembling. She lifted her head. She was crying as well: tears streamed from her eyes. *But I've had a bad time over you*, Nick thought. So his arms remained stiff by his sides. He would give nothing away until he was sure where he stood.

"I was Margie's best friend," she sniffed between sobs.

"I know that."

"She told me everything, about you, about what she felt. She really loved you."

"Then why did she go with Firs?"

"For you."

"What do you mean?"

Karen looked away from him. She loosed her hold and took a step back. She wiped her eyes with a tissue and then said, "You've got to listen hard now and promise me you won't interrupt."

"All right."

He sat on the short grass and clasped his hands round his knees. After a second's hesitation, Karen sat with him.

"One night at the end of June, you were riding at Chester and wouldn't be back until next day. I asked Margie if she would come with me for the evening into Salebourne. We went to the Zero Club. Some bloke there tried to pick me up. Well, I went for a drink and a dance with him but he was horrible so I was back within an hour. Margie was still where I left her, but this Ted Firs was talking to her. We both knew what a dipstick he was and she didn't look happy, except when she saw me. So I called out to her, 'Margie, we've got to catch our bus now,' and she was out of that place like a shot. He ran after us saying he'd give us a lift but we kept going and soon he gave up. 'He's not just thick, he's nasty,' she said. 'Keep out of his way then,' I answered. 'I can't,' she said. 'He's dangerous as well.' I asked her what she meant. He'd been shouting his stupid mouth off, how he was in some big criminal gang, how he was in the know, how he was going to be part of a big job soon. Well, Margie didn't listen. She thought it was all rubbish. But then he said, 'And that Nick Welsh of yours had better look out. He could soon come to a nasty end. He'll find it's dangerous riding horses for the rich.' She hung on every word he said after that. But he wouldn't tell her more. 'There's only one way you're going to find out,' he said and then he started on his 'What about it, then, girl?' routine. Nick, he was *foul*. But Margie believed him now. She was frightened. She wanted to tell you. I told her not to because she surely couldn't take anything a twerp like that said seriously. 'But I *don't know*,' she said. 'There's only one thing I can do. I'll have to pretend I like him and worm out everything he's talking about.' 'That's dangerous,' I told her. 'It could be more dangerous for Nick,' she answered. Nick, you've got to believe this. She *hated* being near him and she did it for *you*."

Nick couldn't say anything.

"So she started seeing him in Salebourne two evenings a week. She made sure she kept out of his way when she was with you. This went on for about six weeks. During that time he came into all that money, turned up one night in a flashy car wearing his leather pants and wouldn't tell her where he got the money except, 'It's the first instalment from that big job I told you about and there'll be more where this came from.' Margie had to get more out of him and all he would say was that everybody knew he was brilliant with motors (that's a laugh) and he'd done some really important work on one. He let the name 'Kiteley' slip as well – he'd been there. So Margie and me, we tried to sort out what he meant."

Nick spoke for the first time. "That's it," he said. "He worked for Kiteley on that horsebox they used for the switch. So he *was* in on it."

"That must be it," said Karen. "I knew there was something up when they loaded Nemo up that day and brought a horse back which I only caught a glimpse of before he was pushed in the stable. I was sure I saw a white streak on his head, but until you started muttering about the horse you rode not being Sunrise, I never thought any more about it. I looked in the stable next morning – and there was a horse with no stripe. So I thought I'd been mistaken and shut up about it. But when Brown came charging in ordering us to put Nemo on board again, that's when I said to myself, 'the crunch has come'. So I did a little bit of ringing myself."

"But what were you *doing* at Kiteley's?" cried Nick.

"Don't rush me. This is difficult enough," said Karen. "Margie went on seeing Ted and one day she said to me in the shop that she really was beginning to believe some of the things he said and they frightened her. I asked her what it was all about but she didn't know details, only a big plot with shadowy people at the top and big racing scams coming up and how shocked she would be if she knew who the 'Mr Big' – Ted's words – behind it all and who it was all aimed at were."

"So who was it aimed at?"

"She didn't know. Except that Ted said he was connected with *you*. Margie got it into her head that they'd get at this mysterious person by getting at you."

"That's crazy. Unless it meant Kiteley was going to get back at Johnny. We all know he'd have loved to."

"No, something *much* bigger than that."

"Then I don't get it." But then a new thought came. "Wait a minute. Big people. I'm the regular jockey now for Billy Boney's prize horse. That's my longest connection with the rich and famous."

"That's not it. Who'd want to do down a comic? What about Sir Norbury Greyling?"

"But I wasn't Greyling's jockey until after Margie was murdered. *So* how could anyone make a connection?" Then came another thought. "But they *could*. Kiteley was involved. He knows what goes on in racing and how trainers think. Paddy O'Keefe had signed up as his top stable jockey. So he wouldn't be riding Sunrise again. Johnny didn't want him to anyway. So Kiteley would *guess* Johnny would give Greyling's best rides to me." Then puzzlement. "But what's that got to do with it?"

"Well, anyway, Margie was scared stiff for you by now."

And that, Nick thought, *is why she said all those strange things to me by the river which I forgot and never remembered until it was too late.*

Karen was continuing. "She was frightened for you and she was beginning to be frightened for herself as well. Once she asked Ted not to give her any more big talk, and he said, 'You can't stop listening now. We're joined up, you and me. You're as deep in it as I am. If you stop seeing me, I'll put the heavy mob on to shut you up. You know too much.' Well, in a way, she did. But also she knew nothing. She couldn't go to the police, they'd laugh at her. She couldn't tell you – not yet, anyway, there was nothing to tell that you'd take seriously."

"I bet I would," said Nick. But he knew he wouldn't.

"I'll never forget, one day two weeks before she was killed, she said to me, 'Karen, I'm in danger. If Ted's telling half the truth about these people, then he's going to be silenced when they find out. And if he is, then so will I be. But I can't get out of it now.' Nick, it was terrible to listen to her. 'But if I *am* silenced, I want you to look after Nick.' At first, I laughed at her, I remember, and I'm ashamed of that now. But she convinced me. And then I said – it all came to me in a flash – 'Here am I trying to get started at a good stable and be apprenticed as a jockey – why don't I apply to Kiteley to work at his place? He might even send me on the Newmarket course. And if Kiteley's is where it's all happening, then I'll see for myself.' 'Don't tell Nick,' she said. So I never did. Kiteley took me on straight away."

"Why so fast?" said Nick.

"Because he's a dirty old man, that's why. He wanted someone new to leer at. But can you see why I couldn't tell you?"

"I don't know yet," said Nick. "Why did you lie about the Moxons?"

"Because Margie told me what she meant about 'looking after you'. I told her this fixation she'd got about being silenced was morbid, but she wouldn't have it. She said she knew I liked you and I was to try to carry on with you where she would have to leave off. I said, 'Margie, that's a terrible thing to say,' and she said I wouldn't think so when it had happened. So after she was murdered, I thought I'd be letting her down if I didn't keep with you all the time. There was only one way I could think of to take your mind off Margie's death."

"I see," said Nick slowly. "I *think* I understand what you're saying. You were leading a double life, weren't you?"

"Yes, I was."

"But how can I be sure—" Suddenly something else occurred to him. "But that means all you've been saying about how much you feel for me, how you've been getting me going all this time, it's false, you've been making a fool of me."

"Oh, no, Nick," said Karen quietly. "Never that."

"Oh, yes, you have. I see it now. You may have

been doing this for Margie, but it's all a long revenge for what happened that night in the recreation ground." Nick was working himself up into real anger.

Karen stepped back from him. Her voice was suddenly hard. "Why?" she said. "Do you think you *deserve* revenge taken on you for that?"

Nick's anger died. "Yes," he said. "I do."

Karen turned towards him again, put her head on his shoulder. "Then consider the revenge finished. I've never said an untrue word about what I feel for you. You *must* believe that."

Up here on the Downs, in a burgeoning night wind as the moon rose, Nick knew that he did believe it, and always would. And he was aware of Margie, somehow very close, telling him he was right to.

Chase, Kemp and Ruggles waited in an unmarked car in a layby. Opposite was the horsebox, empty but for Kiteley's horse. Unobtrusively in side turnings a few hundred metres either side, police cars waited.

Chase mused over the past events. There was no pattern to them, no rhyme or reason. Four deaths, all of them needless. Margie and Firs because of Firs' big mouth. Ray Ling – well, he must have found out more than was good for him. There was little doubt that the man known as Drake or Brown had killed them. And the body in the reeds? Chase would bet good money it was the real Drake, on his way to Matley.

But what now? The plan was blown.

Plan? What plan? A horse faked for one race? The switch should have happened at Buckingham, but after Firs blabbed it must have been postponed until Stortford. Why? If the favourite was ringed to fix a race, there would surely be a sudden surge of betting against it. But there wasn't. Why not? What was the point of it all?

Well, Mornington Sunrise was back in his stable so they would never know. Nick Welsh and Karen Thorpe between them had put him there.

A very nasty thought crept into Chase's mind. *Unless this habitual killer who seemed to glory in leaving a trail of bodies behind was caught, they could be next.*

But if the plan was blown, its aim had been foiled. What was that aim? There must have been some climax, finale, set for the near future.

There was only one possibility. The season's final classic. The St Leger at Doncaster. Mornington Sunrise would run. So how would the plan have worked?

Ruggles in the driver's seat nudged him. A taxi had stopped by the horsebox. A dark figure got out, paid the driver. Chase spoke softly into the radio.

"White Ford Mondeo taxi leaving, travelling north. Stop it and hold the driver for questioning."

The tall figure paused, looked up and down the road, saw nothing suspicious. He must have thought a commercial traveller was having a nap in the opposite layby. He opened the driver's door of the horsebox.

"Be ready to intercept the horsebox," Chase said into the radio. Ruggles switched the headlights on and drove across the road, blocking the horsebox in. Chase got out, half expecting a gun to be levelled at him. But instead, the door opened and a man climbed down. It seemed almost as if he was glad to be arrested.

"I should have known it," said Chase. "Mr Soames, I believe."

At Salebourne police station, Soames talked a lot. Yes, he took calls from Drake every night, but no, they were not what Sir Norbury thought they were. Soames had been targeted by this man Brown and blackmailed. No, his name might not be Brown. But it certainly wasn't Drake. Drake had been a good man – ex-paratrooper, ex-Horse Guards, helicopter pilot, brave, trustworthy. Soames had grieved that he had knowingly sent him to his death that day Sir Norbury sent him to Matley. Because Soames passed the news on at once and knew what the outcome would be.

No, Brown was a terrifying man. He knew how to play on people's weaknesses and make them his slaves: Soames through blackmail, Kiteley through greed and his hatred of Johnny. Brown had entered their lives an unstoppable force.

But why?

Soames thought hard.

"I've often wondered what the true aim of all this

elaboration was. There's only one possibility. It's aimed at Sir Norbury."

"Have you any quarrel with Sir Norbury?"

"None. It is Brown I am frightened by."

"Then why tell us? Brown is free. You know he kills indiscriminately. What price will your life be worth?"

Soames shuddered. "I'll tell you all I know in return for protection and leniency."

Chase made no comment. "Was Brown on his own?" he said. He was thinking of Sir Norbury Greyling's feared and mysterious brother Kenton. Could *he* be Brown?

"I know this," said Soames. "There was someone behind him, someone of whom even Brown seemed frightened. Just once, when he referred to 'the boss'."

"Who was this boss?"

"I don't know. But if he worried Brown, then I don't want to meet him."

Silence. Chase changed tack.

"So your only part in this was to sit at Scallon Manor by the phone?"

No answer.

"Mr Soames, you want our help. You must tell us all you know."

Silence again.

"There have been four murders," said Chase. "By telling Brown that Drake was on his way to Matley, you have made yourself an accessory to one. If you want help, you will have to tell us all about the others."

Soames sighed. "All right," he said heavily.

"I'm waiting," said Chase.

"I know about the first two. Kiteley told Brown that some fool who'd done work for him had got wind of something and was making two and two make five in Salebourne pubs and clubs. Brown made me go with him, to this ghastly club in Salebourne. We kept our ears open to everybody. It wasn't hard to find whose mouth was open the loudest. He must have found out the plan to substitute the horse for the Buckingham meeting. He and his girlfriend left the club. We followed. We stopped them in the car park just as they were getting into his car. We bundled them into the van we'd brought with us and drove to Kiteley's, me following in the man's Capri. I was scared enough of Brown before; tonight I realized just what sort of fiend he was. We drove inside the garage at the stables and made them get out. The man was snivelling with fear. The girl, I remember, was very calm. Brown picked up a big spanner. He said to the man, 'You can run away if you like.' The man sobbed with joy and turned to run. Brown lifted the spanner and killed him with one blow. The girl was about to scream, but Brown clamped his hand over her mouth. He said, 'You should choose better boyfriends.' Then he strangled her. I could not believe what I was seeing. He had a sheet in the back of the van. He made me wrap the girl's body in it. Then we put both in the van. He started laughing. 'I know what we'll do with them,' he said. We left the Capri in the garage and rode out to the Downs, to where Brown said he'd give Sir Norbury's trainer a shock. It would please Kiteley. So we tipped her out there, where the horses would run in the morning. It was then that he must have had just a twinge of doubt. He mentioned his boss for the one and only time. Brown had been through the man's pockets and had found his name and address. So we headed back into Kiteley's, picked up the Capri, drove back into town, explored the road where he lived and he worked out some rigmarole for us to leave the body in his back garden so people would think he was sleeping off a hangover. He thought this was very funny."

Chase listened in silence. Then, "Do the names Nick Welsh and Karen Thorpe mean anything to you?"

Soames thought. "Thorpe, no. Welsh – yes. Mornington Sunrise's jockey."

"Not then, he wasn't."

"But Brown said Kiteley knew he would be. It wasn't hard to find out he was the real boyfriend of the girl Brown killed. Brown thought this was funny too. He said to me, 'We'll scare the great new prospect so much he'll never ride a horse again.'"

"It didn't work," said Chase. "What about Ray Ling?"

"He was sniffing round too much for Brown's

liking. Brown thought he'd cottoned on to why they stopped at the services on the way to Stortford. So he got rid of Ling."

"And tried to frame Welsh?"

"Nothing so crude. It was just to give Welsh another shock."

"He has a very unpleasant sense of humour," said Chase.

"That's what I'm afraid of."

Chase ignored that. "I'll want you to write out a statement," he said. "Meanwhile, Bertram Soames, I am arresting you…"

He noted the relief which passed over Soames's face.

The pursuit had careered onwards for miles. The Rover was stopped at Dover as Kiteley and Connors tried to board a cross-Channel ferry. The Golf was found abandoned. A succession of stolen cars stretched out across England. Then nothing. Whoever Brown was, he had vanished.

"Apart from looking for him, can we put the case to rest?" asked Kemp.

Brown had a boss even he was afraid of. Chase could not forget those words. "No, Sergeant Kemp," he said. "It's not over yet."

20

Nick and Karen together saw Inspector Chase next morning. Karen told him all she had told Nick. Chase listened gravely, then said, "Please bring your suspicions to us in future. You could have shared the fate of three people you knew." Karen looked gloomily at the floor. "Cheer up," said Chase. "It didn't happen and between you, you foiled a very nasty plot."

He in turn told them what happened afterwards and of Soames's confessions. He also told them that Kiteley had spilled the beans as well but had added no more to their knowledge. When he had finished, Nick said, "So what's it all going to lead to?"

"I don't know," Chase replied. "Nothing that I can think of seems worth taking all that trouble."

"So was it all pointless?" asked Karen.

"No," said Chase. "I've not told you everything."

Before, he had no intention of doing what he did next. But in front of him were two young people who were deeply involved, had made the case break for him, were tough and resilient – especially Karen – and who had been in danger long enough to be able to cope with it. He changed his mind. He told them everything about Sir Norbury Greyling's revelations about his brother. Then he waited for their reaction.

"Are you saying Drake was Sir Norbury Greyling's *brother*?" cried Nick incredulously.

Chase waited for Nick to insist his own fantasies must be right – that it must be Billy Boney. But Nick said nothing. He had been on the point of bursting out with it – then had thought, *What rubbish. Even I couldn't take that*.

"If Sir Norbury wasn't giving me a paranoid fantasy, then who else could it be? But Soames said something interesting. Brown once let slip that there was someone else. 'Just once he talked about his boss,' Soames said. There was somebody behind Drake."

Karen shuddered at the thought of what such a person might be like.

"And Drake has disappeared," said Nick. "So he and his boss are still around."

"Yes," said Chase.

"So that means it's not finished yet."

"Precisely. The enemy forces will regroup. We'll still have a chance to see what this was all about. And there's something else."

"What's that?" said Karen.

"Stay careful. You two could be in bigger danger than ever."

The days leading up to the September meeting at Doncaster passed swiftly. The whole stables mourned Ray. Nick and Mornington Sunrise were reunited; he learned all over again what a marvellous horse he was given charge of. At the same time he got to know Chucklehead better, to realize she might not be the greatest, but that she had it in her to amaze everybody.

One sunny morning he looked at both horses watching him from adjoining stables. *What a privilege to know such creatures*, he thought.

Connie and Johnny were in a strange mood. Kiteley was gone. He would most likely face a long prison sentence. Even if he were acquitted, he would be finished with racing. His stables would be put up for sale. They were shocked that his hatred of them had gone to such lengths. And yet they missed him. They even began to talk hopefully of what sort of enemy might buy the stables.

And now Karen *did* take up Connie's offer and came to work as the first female stable-hand. The first thing she and Connie did together was to apply for the course at the British Racing School.

So, on the surface, life looked as though it could not be better.

* * *

They were both favoured for going to Doncaster. No cadging lifts for Nick; this time he and Karen travelled up in the Range Rover with Connie and Johnny. "I'm keeping an eye on you both," said Johnny. He didn't say for what reason.

They travelled up the morning before the St Leger. Johnny had horses running on both days. They arrived mid-morning and checked in at a hotel near the course so Nick was ready to ride China Chimneys again in the 2.45.

Not only did he thus get to know the wide, flat, left-handed course but he managed to steer China Chimneys to a respectable third, and get a grudging incline of the head from the Duke of Rothley. "Daft git," he said to himself. "Let him ride his own horses if that's how he feels."

St Leger day dawned bright and clear. Crowds were slowly pouring out of the railway station, lines of cars came up the A1, M18 and along the Bawtry road to the Town Moor course. Nick's stomach tightened at the sight. He'd had many days to remember in the past weeks but this, as far as his career was concerned, would be the finest.

Someone else was in Doncaster that night. The hunch about a climax at Doncaster would not leave Inspector Chase's mind. He deserved leave; despite his wife's annoyance, he decided to spend part of it on his own at the races.

As he drove north he pondered again on the

biggest conundrum of all. It was *leaving* the bodies all over the place – going out of his way to make them be found, in fact – which had foiled Brown. *Why had a resourceful criminal done this?*

Or, put it another way, was Kenton Greyling, wherever he was, *mad* to give such instructions? Another thing. The only reason for the whole scam, a betting coup, had gone. Mornington Sunrise's return to his stable was headline news. He was favourite again now the poor run at Stortford had been discounted. Nobody could make an illegal fortune from him any more. So perhaps his errand was a wild-goose chase and he could enjoy the racing. *Enjoy* the racing? He remembered how he had felt about it at the start of this case. And, in spite of it all, here he was... Well, it must be the horses themselves. And some of the people. He'd certainly changed his mind quite a lot.

Chase had wangled himself a pass to the paddock. He'd see what was going on from close to.

By now, Nick knew his racing afternoons by heart. Chucklehead in the first race, then Mornington Sunrise for the big one. Chucklehead was up against some good horses here, but Nick felt confident as he walked her down to the start. Besides, a win here would make sure Billy Boney's fees were paid for years ahead.

He was drawn in the middle. Chucklehead was tense, as if she could not wait to feel Doncaster's firm green turf under her hooves. And when the starting gate flew up, Nick knew she was feeling good. For the first four furlongs she was tucked neatly in fourth, letting the others do the work. Grey-eyed Monster was three lengths clear by the halfway stage; Nick saw the jockey using his whip already, though, and guessed the horse would never make it. Five furlongs from home he made his move. Chucklehead advanced from fourth to second. The toiling Grey-eyed Monster, who had been lying second, was passed. Only Spiky Pumpkin remained in front. A furlong out and Nick eased Chucklehead into her final burst. She took Spiky Pumpkin ten lengths out and won by a length.

Nick was so pleased – for himself, for this super, improving mare, but most of all for Billy Boney. Once again the comic was there, almost pathetically overjoyed. He pumped Nick's hand, embraced the horse and crooned "You little darling" over and over again so Nick had no idea which one of them he meant.

And how pleased everyone was round him. Karen was there, seeing herself in years to come. Johnny clapped Nick on the shoulder and said, "I knew I'd backed a good'un in you. You make an ordinary horse look great." And who else should be there, to Nick's surprise, but Sir Norbury Greyling, sharing Billy Boney's triumph, it seemed, while waiting for what everybody hoped would be his own. Nick looked at the two together for the first time. Chalk and cheese.

"My congratulations, sir," Sir Norbury said to Billy. "But do I have to call you Boney?"

"Billy will do," said Billy.

"Well, whatever it is, I hope we can share a double celebration soon."

No flicker of recognition. They could not possibly be connected.

Karen thought she had never seen so different a pair together as the tycoon and the comedian. Yet, inspired by one success and the prospect of another, the differences between them were as nothing. They were just racing folk, like she was.

Chase, standing in the paddock some way off, had noticed this sudden blooming friendship. Good, he thought. It would be a way of laying Nick's obsession to rest for ever. Standing here in the paddock on his own, though, was not good enough. He wished he could get nearer, in with the owners and trainers.

Johnny was just within hailing distance. "Mr Rumbold-Straight," Chase called.

Johnny heard and came over. "Inspector Chase," he cried genially. The police had gone up somewhat in his estimation. "Come and join us. Duck under the rails. I'll answer for you. You're my guest."

No, Johnny plainly had no idea the danger might not yet be over and Chase decided not to tell him.

Nick knew Paddy O'Keefe was riding Artificial Cream in the St Leger and was second favourite.

He'd tried to catch a word in the weighing-in room, but Paddy was concentrating on his own business. Only when their horses were walking down to the start could he draw level and speak.

"So how's Kiteley's arrest going to affect you?" he said.

O'Keefe shrugged his shoulders. "Bad business," he said. "I'm sorry. I never liked him, though I rode for him. But I've been paid my retainer and life goes on so here I am today."

He ruffled Artificial Cream's mane. "It's about time I gave this up. Racing's getting to be a trial now. I've made a good pile. I might buy the stables myself." He turned and looked at Nick shrewdly. "Remember what you said to me at Bishop's Stortford? My turning up next door might test your loyalty! Good luck, mate."

"And you," said Nick.

O'Keefe spurred Artificial Cream on with his heels and the horse cantered away.

Now they were in the stalls at the start. There was a short spur before the horses reached the wide, pear-shaped course with its left-handed bends. Then there was a full circuit before the final straight to the winning post, placed just before they would have reached the first and tightest bend for the second time. Nick had received a good high draw. *Everything's in my favour. If I can't win today, I'm worthless*, he thought. Artificial Cream, though, was drawn next to him. So it would be an equal contest.

He had no advantage over his rival.

Mornington Sunrise was calm as usual. But Nick felt his own heart beating fast. This was the crunch, the biggest racing test of his life.

They were in the stalls under starter's orders. Suddenly, they were off. At once, Nick knew Sunrise was at his best, galloping easily within himself on the lovely surface of the Town Moor course. Along the first straight he lay third. Artificial Cream he could not see, but was quite sure Paddy would be tucked in very close. Mornington Sunrise did not check round the first sharp bend under the stands and moved up a place. Out into the country now and the long sweeping bends until the final straight. O'Keefe would have to make his move soon. He must know he could not afford to let Sunrise stay ahead of him, the one horse who could take any other horse in the race whenever he wanted to.

Just round the last bend, six furlongs to go, and there he was. The crouched jockey on the big grey horse surged past, took the lead, opened up a three length gap.

But Nick bided his time, even letting Sunrise bide his own time. For two furlongs, Artificial Cream kept up the gap. Then, as before at Buckingham, Nick felt the same gather of strength, the smooth acceleration, the knowledge that nothing would stop him winning his first classic.

No sudden veer, no clever riding tactics from Paddy could have the slightest effect. Mornington

Sunrise passed the now toiling grey and finished two lengths clear.

Chase felt the excitement. But he was not part of it. He watched Karen and Alf lead Sunrise into the unsaddling enclosure, felt the joy of Connie and Johnny, saw Sir Norbury shaking Nick by the hand and then loop his arm round Billy Boney's shoulders as they both laughed and danced like little boys, not two men at the very summits of their respective but wildly different callings. The supreme businessman and the supreme comic, connected only by racing. It was somehow comforting to see their pleasure together, after weeks of trying to solve a mystery which was itself like a series of sick jokes.

A series of sick jokes. Chase felt suddenly cold. *Of course.* Everything that had happened since Margie's death was like a sick joke. The joke was that a secret conspiracy was advertised so the world knew about it every inch of the way. The sickness was that the advertising consisted of four very cold-blooded murders. There was a *horrible* sense of humour behind it all.

Whose? Chase looked again at the ill-assorted pair. One burly, thickset, the other lanky, a beanpole. One with a serious face with a turned down mouth; the other with mobile features, a mouth which didn't need make-up to push the lips into a sudden smile after the mock depression which made millions adore him. Like the twin masks of tragedy and comedy. And now Chase was hit by a sudden lightning bolt of understanding. *Nick was right. The two faces were the same.*

Sir Norbury was afraid of his brother. Who was his brother?

Chase felt the hunch start from his feet, move upwards until his whole body shook and tingled. He turned his back on the celebrating crowd, took out his mobile phone and dialled. The Matley incident room had been stood down now, he got straight through to Salebourne and Kemp.

"Billy Boney. What do we know about his early life?"

"Not a lot. He's always been cagey about his beginnings. Part of his charm, I suppose."

"Find out everything you can."

He would have to take Nick seriously after all.

21

The presentation was over. Nick left the unsaddling enclosure, acknowledged the congratulations of other jockeys, said the obligatory few words to TV and radio commentators, and rushed away to shower and change.

On went his new shirt, slacks and loafers bought for the occasion. More formal wear would come later. He prepared to join the others in Sir Norbury's private box. But before he could go, Paddy O'Keefe stopped him.

"Nick," he said. "You did superbly. My congratulations."

He held his hand out. Nick shook it gladly.

"That's my last classic," said Paddy. "I'm past it. I'll leave it to you now."

Nick was at a loss for words. Strangely, there was a lump in his throat.

Paddy continued. "All these years I've carried a little good luck charm. I want you to have it."

He fished in his pocket and produced something metal and shining. For a moment, Nick didn't know what it was.

"My trusty knuckleduster," said Paddy. "Here, fit it on your hand."

He slipped it over the fingers of Nick's right hand. Nick closed his fist. Suddenly he felt very powerful.

"An old Irish jockey gave it me when he retired," said Paddy. "I guess he may have had to use it. I never did. But it was my lucky charm and I took it to every meeting I ever rode in. Now I'll pass it on. Make sure you give it to some young sprog when your turn comes."

Nick was speechless. He knew this was a big moment in his career.

Paddy turned and walked away. "See you in Matley," he called over his shoulder. "Make sure you ride for me."

"Thanks," was all Nick could stutter. He wished he could say more. Instead, he went to join the others.

The celebrations had started. Sir Norbury had noticed Chase there then and had expansively insisted that he join them. Chase knew he had to keep a clear head. So, he noticed, did Karen and the newly-arrived Nick.

Sir Norbury was at the toasting stage. "Raise your glasses," he said. Chase grasped his orange juice, Nick and Karen their Diet Cokes. "I give you my excellent trainer and his wife, their efficient staff, my wonderful new jockey and his young lady. I give you my fellow owner who has shared a triumph with me today. And, most of all, I give you our horses. We have come through great tribulation to reach today unscathed. But it has all been worth it. So here's to our latest and most welcome guest, the intrepid policeman who has made it all possible. To you all."

Nothing has been worth what's happened, thought Chase as he joined in the reply, "To us all."

"And now," said Sir Norbury. "We should eat. But I have a fancy not to eat here. I have a better idea."

Everybody looked at him expectantly. After all, he was the one best able to pay.

"The food here is good but the food at Scallon Manor is better. I have already telephoned André, my chef, and my staff are alerted. I invite you all on my private helicopter waiting at the local airport. We will be home in under two hours. I am sure you can wait that long for true culinary delight."

Chase was surprised. He was included in the invitation, so he would be able to keep a watch on Billy Boney. It was his duty, after all. What about his car, left in the car park? Someone could come up and collect it. As soon as he could, he unobtrusively rang Kemp again to let him know the new plan.

"We're all going on his private helicopter. Yes, I know, it must be a big one. We'll be landing at Scallon Manor, he says, in about two hours. I'll keep in touch."

Kemp put the phone down. He told Ruggles.

"There's a surprise," said Ruggles. "Nice for the boss, though."

"Yes," said Kemp musingly. "A big surprise."

He dialled a number – the prison where Soames was on remand. "I want to speak to Mr Soames," he said. "Urgently."

Chase put his phone back in his pocket and waited for what could either be a big treat or a big revelation.

Nick had never felt so supremely happy. Everything was coming together. Every moment was to be savoured. Yet, as Karen squeezed his hand, and he looked at her clear-eyed face and knew what a treasure she had been, he only longed for the day to be over so he could be alone with her.

Sir Norbury called for taxis to take them to Doncaster airport. There, amid the private jets of other rich owners, stood his own Bell Twin Ranger, built for two pilots and five passengers.

"Don't worry," said Sir Norbury. "We can squeeze an extra person in."

Excitedly, they trooped on board. Only momentarily did Chase have any twinge of doubt. Even so, as they walked across the tarmac, he had managed a quick call to Salebourne, "Now boarding Bell helicopter." He gave its number. "Destination Scallon Manor. Keep track of us."

Now they were all sitting in the surprisingly comfortable cabin. Sir Norbury, happier than anyone had ever seen him, had expansively welcomed everybody aboard. But there had been one cloud over his face. He had spotted Chase's phone. "I must have that," he said. "You must know they should never be used in aircraft." *Of course I know*, Chase thought. But he handed it over – why start a row?

The rotors were turning. The engine chattered into life. They rose. Nick and Karen watched delightedly as the racecourse, the town of Doncaster, the railway works, the flat Yorkshire countryside spread out beneath them. They all settled down to a quiet flight.

But no, Sir Norbury had not finished yet. He had not sat down. He stood and faced them all. Beside him sat the pilot, helmeted and anonymous. Sir Norbury was about to speak.

"I'm so pleased to welcome friends both new and old aboard my favourite transport," he said. "And especially the Inspector, so assiduous in the investigation of the recent terrible events. We all give our thanks to him."

Chase was embarrassed as Sir Norbury started clapping and, one by one, the others clapped too. The scene, he thought, was quite ridiculous. However, Sir Norbury had not finished with him.

"When I last saw the Inspector, I set him a task. Sadly, he never finished it. But I did."

Everyone looked wonderingly at Chase. Sir Norbury continued.

"I asked him to discover my long-lost brother. Find him, I said, and you'll solve the mystery. While he dithered, *I have done his job*."

Chase sat bolt upright. Nick and Karen stopped looking out of the window. Connie and Johnny looked as if, fascinating though this all was, it had nothing to do with them. Billy Boney sat looking straight ahead.

Suddenly, Nick knew. He sprang up.

"I'm right," he shouted at Chase. "They *are* connected. You should have listened to me."

Sir Norbury continued as if the interruption had never been made.

"Yes, I have made new enquiries. And I have found the answer. My brother, who I have not seen for thirty years, who disappeared from my life into oblivion, is on board with us now. He is my fellow racehorse owner, Mr Billy Boney."

He gestured towards Billy like a conjuror completing a particularly difficult trick. He did not appear to notice that Nick and Chase could not look surprised.

"Did you know that, Mr Boney? Or dear Kenton, as I should say?" said Sir Norbury.

"Yes, of course I did," muttered Billy. "But we agreed…"

"*Agreed?*" shouted Sir Norbury. "Funny sort of agreement, if I may say so."

So Nick's obsession was not bizarre but triumphantly right, thought Chase.

Nick was thinking, *Why didn't I go to the Inspector*

after Buckingham and the first time I thought of it?
Would Ray have been murdered?

"So I have to cast a shadow over our happy gathering," said Sir Norbury. "For the Inspector will wish to arrest you the moment we land."

Well, yes, he should. But Chase was unhappy. This unfolding scene was unreal; it didn't ring true.

Billy Boney stood, his mouth working. "I never wanted anyone to know," he gasped. "But that's no reason to arrest me."

"Oh, be reasonable, Kenton," said Sir Norbury. "You know as well as I do or the Inspector does that you're behind all the murders and the attempt to switch Mornington Sunrise."

"That's ridiculous," Billy burst out. "Why me?"

"Because you need the money from a really gigantic betting coup so much. Because you have unsavoury friends. Because you hit on a wonderful plan to abduct your brother's horse and substitute its inferior double. The two bad results would lengthen the price so much that by the time you had restored the horse, switched it again for the St Leger and it undoubtedly won, you would have so many bets placed anonymously all over the country that the result would be a considerable fortune. But it all went wrong. So, sadly for you, no long prices and no fortune."

Billy Boney sat in his seat, mouth open, gasping, lost for words. Sir Norbury now had a beatific smile on his face.

"Now, Inspector Chase, I have done your duty for you. I wonder sometimes why we spend our rates and taxes on a police force when we can do the job just as well ourselves. But there's one thing I can't do, which I must leave to you. Arrest this man, please."

Chase did not move. He spoke. "Sir Norbury, I know your theory fits the statement you made to me. But I must certainly have more proof before I do such a thing."

"Proof?" shouted Sir Norbury. "There's proof all round you. Who else has such a hatred of me that he could say 'You will lose the will to live?' Who else has such a weird sense of humour that he can cause a trail of bodies to be left for anyone – no, *one person* – to find, for no other reason than to pass messages to me that I am at the end of this deathly chain? What is it all but one big, macabre joke?"

Chase knew he had told himself the person behind this must have a strange sense of humour. Yes, Sir Norbury could be right. But there was something else. *Where was his hunch now?* It had disappeared. He saw Billy Boney a pathetic sight reduced to gasping pulp and he *knew* it wasn't true.

So what was he to do?

Nick was listening to all this dumbstruck, like everyone else. Karen's look was intent as if she was watching a riveting play. Nick turned to her – and realized she was not looking at Sir Norbury, but straight ahead, staring at the back of the pilot's head.

Now she looked away. Her face was puzzled.

"Nick," she whispered. "The pilot. The way his shoulders hunch up. I've seen them before. It's the man who ordered us to load Nemo into the horsebox."

"You mean Drake. Don't be daft. He's on the run."

"No, I'm sure."

"I'm going to look." Nick stood up and pushed his way to the front. Sir Norbury barred his way.

"Sit down."

"I want to see the pilot. I think I know him."

"SIT DOWN!"

"All right." Nick did so. But only because, close to, he had seen enough.

"Inspector," he called out. "The pilot is Drake."

It took Chase a few moments to work out the possible significance of this fact.

"Sir Norbury, can you introduce us to your pilot?"

"My pilot? A trusted employee."

"And not a multiple murderer on the run?"

"Ah," said Sir Norbury. "If you say so. Another triumph for my twisted brother, insinuating his accomplice into my humble transport."

His eyes glittered, his mouth split into a wide grin.

Nick, Karen and Chase made the realization at the same time.

"He's off his head," said Karen.

"He's barking mad," cried Nick.

"You're more than paranoid. You're insane," said

Chase, levelly.

Johnny gasped with horror. "How can you say that? This is Sir Norbury Greyling you're talking to."

"Johnny," said Chase gently. "I think you're a better judge of horses than people."

Billy found his voice. "Norbury, what are you saying about me?"

And now obsession returned to Nick stronger than ever, though turned completely upside down. Suddenly the whole mystery was clear to him. This *was* a war between two brothers – but the other way round. *Sir Norbury* was behind it, *Sir Norbury* had caused Drake to commit the murders, to make the switch – of his own horse. *Sir Norbury* would be the unknown buyer of Sunrise's twin. Drake's mysterious boss whom Soames would not like to meet was, by supreme irony, his boss already.

"It's not Billy who did it all," he shrieked. "It's him."

Chase stood up. Sir Norbury was quiet, biding his time. Chase spoke. "Nick's right. What you've told us is a perfect mirror of the truth, isn't it? *You* started this, *you* wanted the bodies left unhidden to cause the greatest upset, to make it plausible your brother sought to frighten you. You even sent your own Drake to his new job knowing that he would be intercepted and murdered on the way. You caused your own horses to be switched. Why go to such ridiculous lengths?"

Sir Norbury burst into laughter. "You're so clever,

Inspector. But I've already told you why. Billy would win a fortune. But then he would be caught. I'd make sure of that. So he would be ruined. Nobody then could make me lose the will to live."

Nick burst out. "You'd have ruined me, too, with that inquiry. But I don't think you'd have gone through with it. It was just a blind. You'd have had no one else to ride Sunrise like me."

"What a very perceptive young lad you are. Not just a good jockey. Well, you all seem to have made up your minds."

He surveyed them all.

"Strange to relate, you're all quite correct," he said. "Inspector, what I told you the other day was true – about my brother, I mean. I feared him, I hated him – and he really did say those terrible words to me as he left for ever to go on his way. I believe we both aspired as high as we could in our respective fields just to spite the other, to send each other messages – 'I'm too good at what I do so don't mess with me.' I knew who he was all the time. I was not frank with you about that, Inspector. We had years ago agreed to keep our relationship secret. It would not help either of our images. But have you any idea how a phrase like 'You will lose the will to live' preys on the mind? Every business triumph, every notch up the ladder I made, I heard him saying it. For years and years until it could no longer be borne. 'Kenton,' I said. 'I must make you lose *your* will to live.' How? By ruining him in the public eye. By making them think he was behind not just a swindle but a series of murders. Once I thought of that, the whole plan fell into place so easily. Brown I recruited – not his real name, of course – soldier of fortune, supremely competent, who'd shrink from nothing. Our first two murders were born of necessity. It was a good plan of Brown's to leave one in the path of Johnny's horses. Who it was and who found her nearly constituted our most brilliant stroke. Though perhaps in the long run it proved to be not so fortunate. Only the accident of Nick Welsh being where he had no business foiled it all at the last."

He stopped as if considering.

"Yes, my plan is ruined," he said. "But I can't let it be made known. That's why you are all here, in one place, where I have brought you. I've won my great race with my great horse. That's one triumph. Now for the next. Not the one I wanted but good enough."

Chase felt a sinking of the heart.

"I'm afraid we've played a trick on you, Brown and I. We'll be landing at Scallon Manor very soon now. And he and I will get out of the helicopter. But you, I fear, won't. Oh, dear, how these doors jam sometimes. You see, there's a bomb on board. We will be gone, you will be trapped in here. Five minutes for us to get well clear, and there'll be no one left to tell the story of my little plan. Brown will be well paid and then out of my sight for ever. But for you – the end of the road, I fear. Not the true revenge outcome I wanted. But you all got in the way so much that you only have yourselves to blame."

He stopped talking. The only sound was the throb–throb of the engines. Yes, now everyone could see for themselves. Sir Norbury Greyling, top of the capitalist tree, was certifiably mad. And with it, appallingly clear-headed.

Nobody could move. The engine note changed. They were dropping. Chase recognized Scallon Manor below. Johnny stood as if to grapple with Sir Norbury. But Sir Norbury produced a small, shining revolver from his pocket – an action so out of character, thought Chase.

"Don't reduce what speck of life you still have," said Sir Norbury. "While there's life, there's hope, after all."

He stepped back. He pressed a button. There was now a sealed barrier of steel lattices between cabin and cockpit. The noise of the rotors changed. They were descending.

Nick was really staring death in the face now, not just skirting round it. He looked up at Karen, saw those clear eyes. He thought of Margie. Then he thought of the sheer, all-enveloping delight when Mornington Sunrise passed the winning post and he had won so early – yet so late – in his career one of the great classics of British racing. Well, he'd had more good times in the last six months than most people had in a lifetime. And he found that, now the moment was here, he was calm. Fearful, yes, but thinking straight and knowing he was with good people. Poor consolation, but something.

Johnny was too angry to be frightened. "Damned owners," he raved. "They've mucked up my life and now they're the death of me." Even now he was purely a trainer. And Connie, despite her own panic, smiled at him.

Billy Boney was slumped, almost unconscious, while Chase was wondering if there had been any way, among the numerous permutations he had considered, he could have thought of this and guarded against it.

The helicopter gently touched the ground. The rotors slowed, stopped. The pilot stood. He turned and looked through the barrier.

Drake. Or Brown.

"Goodbye to you all, my friends," said Sir Norbury. He looked at his watch. "Your wait will be exactly five minutes. We will be so amazed at our luck in being thrown clear, so distraught at our inability to save you. And I have already posted letters as if from terrorist organizations claiming responsibility for the bomb. Why, I have even placed one on the Internet. Poor Sir Norbury, losing all his new friends and, worst of all, his long-lost brother."

They were gone. The silence was eerie. Johnny first tried to wrench at the steel lattices of the barrier, then pull a seat out, then take off his shoe and beat uselessly with a heel against the window. Chase examined the barrier more calmly, then the rear hatchway, then the roof. Everything was secure.

Suddenly the cabin was filled with a collective despair.

Chase broke the silence. "Four and a half minutes to go. It's no use waiting. We have to try to get out."

"What's the use?" groaned Johnny. "You can't escape from a pressurized cabin."

"But this won't be pressurized. Helicopters don't fly that high," said Chase. "We could break a window."

"What with? You can bet your life he's removed all the fire-fighting equipment," said Johnny.

The quiet of despair again.

Then Nick had a thought, unexpected, irrelevant, useless.

Lucky Paddy, having a lucky charm he never had to use the way it was meant to be. I'd rather be in a fight with ten hob-nailed hoodlums than here...

Then the merest ray of sunshine: *but I could use it.*

He took Paddy's knuckleduster out of his pocket. It gleamed, as if to say, "Go on, try me." Then he looked at the window, thick, tough, probably impregnable.

"I've got something," he said.

He fitted Paddy's knuckleduster over his fingers. Well, why not try? It *could* work. And if it didn't...

"Three and a half minutes," said Chase.

Nick bunched his fist, then smashed at the laminated glass. The glass stayed unmarked.

"Three minutes," said Chase.

Again, smash, smash, smash, to no avail.

"Two and a half minutes," said Chase.

No good. We're finished. Nick took a final swing of blind, frustrated anger at the window.

The slightest of changes. The glass shivered, crazed, cracked with painful slowness.

"Two minutes," said Chase.

"It's going," cried Nick.

Smash, smash again. Bigger crazes crossed the surface.

"Here, let me push," said Chase. Johnny joined, then Billy, Karen and Connie. The window moved, bellied outwards, burst. The way, miraculously, was clear. There was sudden frenetic scrambling; they dropped to the ground under the now still rotors and ran for their lives to escape any blast. Blindly they pounded over the short grass.

The explosion ripped through the air when they were all a hundred metres away. They threw themselves to the ground. The blast and the shock waves buffeted their prone bodies and scoured their eardrums.

After three minutes of shocked silence, Nick stood up. He wiped sweat from his eyes and blinked. He was staring at a reassuring figure he knew who had loomed up in front of him.

"Take it easy," said Sergeant Kemp. "I won't book you for carrying an offensive weapon."

Nick looked down at his bloodstained, smarting hand, still with the knuckleduster on.

"Paddy's lucky charm," he managed with difficulty to say. "Tested for real at last. Us jockeys stick together."

Never had fresh air, sun, green grass, seemed so blessedly desirable. Police cars were all round them. At the very edge of his blurred vision he was aware of Sir Norbury and Brown being hustled into separate cars by armed policemen.

Kemp turned to Inspector Chase. "Well, we got here," he said.

"Just about," Chase replied. Then, as if ashamed of his churlishness, "How did you know?"

"A hunch. Like yours. We were doing what you asked – boning up on Billy Boney, as you might say. Then you rang to say you were getting on Greyling's helicopter. I thought that if Greyling had his own helicopter, he'd have his own helicopter pilot. Well, I remembered Soames told us the real Drake had been a helicopter pilot. I just wanted to know who'd taken his place. So I spoke to Soames. Yes, Drake had been, no, Greyling hadn't got a new one after Drake had left for Matley and he couldn't see how he'd have got one he would be confident of in the few days Soames had been away. I asked if he would hire one temporarily. Soames said he'd be surprised. He didn't trust what he called 'mercenaries' to do jobs like flying his helicopter. Anyone working for him had to be known through and through and show complete loyalty. Why, he even disliked flying on airlines."

"So?" said Chase.

"Well, it set alarm bells ringing in my mind. I asked Soames if Brown, with all his other talents, could fly helicopters. 'Yes,' he said. 'I know it for a fact.' So I thought – if he could infiltrate the stables and take us all in, why not Scallon Manor? Greyling might not see through him either. And it was possible he could have you all hostage. It was a real surprise to see him and Greyling together. So we took them both. Greyling lost his nerve. He told us about the bomb. I can't begin to tell you how we felt when we saw you escaping."

"But you didn't know enough to justify an armed reaction squad, surely?" said Chase.

"The Superintendent thought so," Kemp replied. "He took it very seriously."

"What can I say?" Chase was amazed as well as full of gratitude.

"You're not the only one with intuition," said Kemp.

Nick could think of only one thing. "Is it really over now?"

"I think that must be the lot," said Chase. "I can't see any loose end. Some things to explain, perhaps – but we'll do that and then the courts can sort it out."

For people who had just escaped death, the little group were in very good shape. Perhaps the shock would come later.

"What about Billy?" said Karen.

Billy Boney's eyes were open now. But he was still speechless. Until he managed one sentence. "Funny sort of brotherly reunion that turned out to be."

"Billy," said Nick, "you stand to be a very rich comedian."

"Don't want it," said Billy. "I'd rather sweat for my pennies."

And so would I, Nick thought. He could do with a lot more days which started as this one had. But no more, please, of such endings. He looked at Karen. She looked at him.

"Yes, it's us two now," he said. "But I'll never forget Margie."

"I don't want you to. And neither will I," Karen answered as they kissed.

Johnny, very pale and still shaking, had risen to his feet. No matter, he would always put first things first.

"That's enough of that," he called out. "Just make sure your passport's ready when you get home. It's France next for you. Mornington Sunrise in the Arc de Triomphe."